FES IS A MIRROR

a novella

CHANTAL JAMES

Willow Books, a Division of AQUARIUS PRESS
Detroit, MI

Contents

For my mother, my father, and Reda

FES, MOROCCO, DECEMBER 1990

I.
BLOOD

…

"I wake you with hundreds
of thousands of volts—
Mic-to-mouth resuscitation."
—Rakim, from "Lyrics of Fury"

1

If You can remember it Sheep, the world is vast and empty.

when i was a boy i used to stay awake at night listening to what was happening in our house—one room where we all slept and ate, lit at night by candles. if you looked at a flame from a candle straight on, unblinking, it danced in rhythm with the voice of whoever was speaking. once in a long while a traveler passed through and i peeked at him shyly as we ate. kept my eyes open that night, rolled up in my rug against one of my brothers, to hear what he had to tell my parents about himself.

and i can remember a man who sold grain speaking with my parents one night, passing through on his way somewhere. he had grown up in the desert too, but far from us. crouched and quiet this night, he said, 'when i was small i thought that my family and the nearest neighboring family were the only people on earth, that no one else existed.' so vast, is the desert. our nearest neighbors, cousins of my father, were an hour's walk over brittle earth; the nearest city, Errachidia, a day away.

somehow prison gives what Fes took away: that feeling i grew up with, that the world was stark. the bareness i didn't know was bare until Fes filled it (with cobblestone. and hooded traffic, and hoofed traffic, someone always shouting, a fight always breaking out (skin against skin)).

You and me, we come from a place where the light from the stars at night is so intentional that you know they are watching you. it's a light so sharp you can hear it, a small sound in a back crease of your ear.

now my days are bare again: there is nothing but me in the whole world. everything that appears in my day is sharp, except those things that lead one dull day into another: the arrival of the same tough crust of bread, the slow increase and decrease of the sun.

from time to time new prisoners come in and out of the cell where they keep me. i search them each with my eyes: tall Congolese stopped on their way to Europe, pickpockets with slick hair, men looking scared and out of place, men looking seasoned and unfazed. sometimes they stay for a few days, sometimes a bit longer, but no one has been here as long as i have. sometimes the one, cold, impossibly damp cell is filled with as many as twenty people, and filled with their smoke, their arguments, their commiseration. i watch, but i tend to keep my distance from them. they have nothing to offer me, mostly.

except for one. it is not my practice to take people as my confidants—only You—but he is good company for a while, and i think i can trust him to go and see about my Sheep. know that i don't stop thinking of You. i know you are helpless without me. i picture You alone and hungry. after all these months i don't know how you're surviving, but i feel that you're alive. can't explain that knowing, but i trust it. like how i know this kid is someone safe to send to You. blood knows blood. the ones who are for you— you feel it. the ones who are not for you: your skin recoils, crawls back on itself. you have to be stripped of everything else, i think, to be able to sense the world like this. being in prison has refined my instincts, returned me to my nature.

city life starts to dull you, and i had forgotten myself in Fes. too much comfort; i'd lost the sharp edge that had helped me rise to my position in the first place, though i didn't know it until i was arrested. if i'd been as sharp on the outside as i am in jail, i never would have ended up here. it's another irony of this position: that prison refines the criminal. and i know that when i get out of here it will be impossible to contain me.

the kid, his name is Rachid. i can tell by looking at him that he's never even been punished by his parents, let alone the law. the build of his body—lean, but soft as a child's—suggests to me that he doesn't stay out in the streets long, and that it's too much thinking that keeps him thin. he looks down his nose at everyone. at first i attributed that to his class, and to his being too sheltered to have imagined himself in a place like this, but when i look at him closer i can see it's something different: it's that he thinks he's too smart. he speaks carefully, like his words are too valuable to be wasted.

he came into the cell and spoke not even a greeting of peace. after some hours, curious about the way he held his body, i threw a pack of cigarettes at him. it hit his shoulder and he winced. he glanced at me quickly, made some kind of quick assessment, and turned his head back to the wall he'd been staring at. the box of cigarettes lay on the cold floor at his side.

'hey Doctor!', i called to him, an offhand nickname to comment on his glasses. it has always been a habit of mine to re-name people. i want you to have to reconsider yourself, when you deal with me. i want there to be a part of you that's mine, a part that i created. this one said, 'Doctor is not my name.'

'save your real name for your mother.' when you're here you safely guard that old person, that free person, because you are hoping for the day when he will walk again. you nourish him in your mind, but keep him to yourself. you keep his record clean.

i was still curious about this new prisoner, and his attitude of defiance. 'my friend,' i offered him, 'smoke a little.'

he opened the box with very careful fingers. he took one out and offered it to me. 'i don't smoke,' i told him, 'but go ahead and please yourself.'

so he took and put it in his own mouth, fished a match out of his pocket, and violently struck it against the wall, a simple act conducted with such anger that it could only have been motivated by fear. for what i could also see about Rachid was that behind his airs he was a very scared young man, and that this fear penetrated every aspect of him at every point in his life, regardless of whether or not he happened to be sitting in a cold, bare jail cell with dangerous people.

he asked me why i carried the box if i didn't smoke. i smiled at him. 'exactly for occasions like this. meeting new friends, helping old ones in need.' the truth is that i discovered a long, long time ago that the only real power is in having something people need. if a man is really at the mercy of something, and you have that thing, then the man's at your mercy. it's exactly where i like to keep other men—at my mercy.

si knew that i had interested this new one in me, because at my words he cocked his head and squinted his eyes, and it opened possibilities in my mind about how he might be useful to me. people are often secretive about themselves, when they're in situations like this; they're trying to preserve their identities, trying to keep the free man inside them safe until he can walk again. but when this Rachid asks me about myself, i am open. i want to build trust with him.

'i am not from Fes,' Aziz tells me, 'i came when i was younger, not more than fifteen.' he is interesting to me. he carries cigarettes but doesn't smoke. i hadn't planned to make friends in this prison, because i know i won't be here for long. i don't really enjoy people like these anyway. i am not one of them. i am here on mistake. i come from a good family. i have clean hands, a bright face. when i pass people like Aziz in the medina i step to the side—people who hold so much tension in their limbs and so much cunning in their glances, people who harbor so much dirt beneath their fingernails. i have never had to sit this close, for this long, to one of them, though i know the medina is full of them nowadays.

when their land had dried, they came to Fes, Aziz among thousands. they came from the countryside. they came from from Imozer, from Azrou, from Ain Luh, from Zraoula, Moujou, Sidi Harazem, Ain Bid Oulad Tayeb, Ain Mersa, Ain Allah. they came, too, from places without names, from the farthest depths of the desert and the highest hidden caves in the mountains. they flooded the old city. they brought their goats to keep chained in the courtyard, their chickens to paw at the roof. they piled cousins upon cousins into decaying old houses, converted apartments, alleyways and alleyways.

they came in a flood, escaping drought. escaping the despair of lying in sand and looking up at the night sky, knowing that both sand and stars go on forever and ever without you, oblivious to all your hopes and ambivalent to your survival. trading sharp dry air and its whisper of smoke for the smell of shit and rotting meat and human bodies under damp clothes. i suppose i even understand them, if i am honest with myself. sometimes, even in Fes, i have felt that same despair, the feeling that you are drowning in the vastness and endlessness of the world. for me it was often a feeling of being buried in history. my family came from Al-Andalus four hundred years ago, where they had been booksellers. they were fleeing the Christian king. they married the sons and daughters of the founders of Fes, who carry the blood of the Prophet, and they built the same house in Fes where i grew up hundreds of years later.

nowadays families like mine are leaving, escaping Fes' decay—as though decay is something you can escape, as though it doesn't have a home in your very body. i have aunts and uncles in Casablanca and Rabat now, who have followed our country's wealth and power there. families like mine are moving to make way for people like Aziz: folks with crust between their fingers, who turn the hallowed arteries of the medina into the hollowed veins of the underworld, who bring crime and violence with them and care nothing for Fes' traditions. as a child i ran my hand along a wall outside, and asked my mother how much older than me the wall was. was it older than her? had it been here forever? 'i'm sure there's someone who knows the age of the walls in Fes,' my mother told me, 'but they are much older than me, almost as old as history itself.'

how crushed i felt when i was small, by history! my city a maze—in which you might turn down an alley, if you had been lost for a while, that could even take you backwards in time. i think this is part of what draws me to Aziz. these days i have been looking for something to comfort me against the feeling that i am so small, and that i can't possibly run fast enough to avoid being erased by time, which stretches endlessly behind me and will always catch up to me, and will end me, to go on unending without me.

i have never in my life considered leaving Fes; it is so infinite that it might as well be the entire world. nor have i ever had the inclination to engage someone like Aziz in conversation—a Berber, a criminal. nor did i ever intend to embark upon this strange adventure, ending up in jail like this. but maybe i have something to gain from this experience, something i wouldn't have thought to choose for myself. maybe i can take with me something to gird me against the feeling that i am helpless, that i am meaningless in the face of everything that has come before me. and maybe it is exactly someone like Aziz—the future of Fes, irreverent of its past—who can offer me some assurance that who i am now matters.

i sit and listen to Aziz and he tells me about himself, where he came from. i have not given him much more than my name. but as he continues i give him my earnest attention. he tells me how You came with him to Fes.

You become a thing in my own head and i wonder about You, if You provide me the escape i so seek, if You can save me as the past never has. i begin to even direct some of my thoughts to You, while You are still an imaginary creature to me. i wonder about your strange origins. then i wonder if a space is opened for us, in the life of someone who doesn't know us, when we think of them.

The first thing Rachid will have me know about him, after his name, is that he won't be here with me for long. he says that his family knows someone in the police force and that enshallah he'll be out in a week.

everything else i need to know about him i can tell just by sitting in the same room, breathing the same air. that he is a university student, for example: he carries this in his bearing, and he is of an age and temperament such that i couldn't imagine another occupation for him. i know too that he feels lost, not just to be sitting here with me in this prison cell, but to have been born into the world. his eyes wander sometimes to nowhere and rest there, unfocused. i know everything about a person without speaking. reading desires has been my business, knowing people where they are weak and wanting, being able to provide them with escape from themselves. but is it only the starkness of prison that sharpens my senses? perhaps it's also that my mind is focused on You these days and that you have always forced me into a place past words. You are wordless. i tell Rachid, 'if you leave me so soon, i want you to see about my Sheep.' 'your herd?,' Rachid asks. 'i am not much of a shepherd.'

'no,' i tell him, 'a person. like my sister. she doesn't speak. she's been with my family since before i came to the city, and i took her with me.'

'but she doesn't speak?'

'no. she isn't like you and me, not as human as we are.'

'is she a spirit?,' Rachid asks. his eyes widen at the idea.

i have nothing to hide from Rachid. i have never hidden in my life. (and if i hid You it was to keep You safe from a world that doesn't love you like i do, and never will.) i suppose some men think that when a man knows about you he owns a part of you, especially in Fes, where you see the same faces everywhere, you walk down the street knowing everything about everyone who passes and knowing that everyone you pass knows everything about you—and that sometimes what somebody knows about you is the only thing he has, his food when he's starving, the weapon he wields to his own advantage. everyone here knows that if news of him reaches the wrong hands, it can be used to destroy him.

but i choose to offer some of myself freely to Rachid, because i know how to use a man's hunger for information against him. you give someone enough of yourself to satiate him, and he is lulled into the sense that he knows you. once he's in that place you can do with him as you want. even if i tell everything about myself i have words to say, so much of who i am remains with me. and i have nothing to lose these days, feeling so far from You and so far from everything i built for myself.

i tell him how i found You, when i still lived in the country. how i was watching my father's herd for him one day when i noticed that a strange animal had wandered among them, a Sheep but not a sheep. naked to the sun, the skin all over your body was chapped and callous, and You walked on all fours. i was just a boy and the sight of You frightened me. i didn't know what you were—something grotesque, a monster, crawling on your knees. outside by the oven, where we fired our bread until it came out rich and brown and full of almost everything our bodies needed, i found my mother's mother, who had strong gnarled arms and could tell the sex of unborn babies.i took her with me back to the herd and she looked at You. You didn't resist her touch. when she lifted You in her arms You gave way easily and limply, and she took You back to the house, me trailing her footsteps. 'it's a girl,' my grandmother told me as i followed her, tumbling over the rocky ground. but You were half-human at best.

it was late September and the sky was charged and itching with lightning, taunting us with the dream of rain. i was ten or so.

'she came to you, Aziz,' my grandmother said, 'so she will sleep beside you.' your body gave off a strong, wild smell. at my grandmother's request i strapped a donkey with two jugs and rode to the well to get water, my legs bouncing against the animal's firm sides. i helped my grandmother bathe You in the yard. your hair was matted and caked with dirt, so we shaved it all off.

then i looked at You and wasn't afraid. You were clean and bald and waited with a sheep's patience, accepting of your fate. your eyes were dull as an animal's—still, when i looked at You directly i saw something almost human. i felt that i'd been charged with You. 'can he be my friend?,' i asked my grandmother. 'she,' my grandmother answered, 'will be like one of us, and we will take care of her.' i decided that i would never let anyone hurt You and that You would be special to me.

You were small enough to be a much younger child, but my grandmother said You were probably around eight years old. strange sounds came from your mouth, like some living thing was struggling out of your throat. these sounds would grow fainter as You stayed with us, fading to silence. You never developed human speech.

my father had been traveling that day, visiting a relative. he came home as the sun was going down to find you wrapped in a blanket, rocking in my grandmother's arms. in a cautious tone of voice, he asked if You were a devil; but my grandmother said that You were from God. and she said you were a human being like the rest of us.

we never sacrificed a sheep to name You like the holy book says. the slow death of the animal You had been was enough. that first night, and for many nights after, my grandmother slowly massaged each of your legs with argan oil, until one day they could unbend completely straight. a year or so later You began to walk, like a person. as your hair grew back, my grandmother kept it combed and braided. and as she had determined, You slept beside me every night. i held You to my body when You were cold. if my brothers and sisters were cruel to You, i stroked your head and whispered things to calm You.

when my grandmother died i was the only one among us that loved You. there were many of us in my family; i had eleven brothers and sisters by the time i left home, and i am sure that more have followed in the years that i've been gone. but draught had settled onto our land like a stubborn flock of angry birds, and had refused to lift for years. what green things there had been on the dry land were shrinking back into the earth. it was harder to feed our family and it was harder to find pasture for our sheep. their numbers dwindled, and many of them began to fall to a disease no one could explain. my father suspected that some magic was being worked against him. we children were becoming more numerous and the strain on our resources was becoming too much.

as long as i can remember, my mother had a baby on her back, tied with a broad, colored piece of cloth. even when she was pregnant, there was a baby on her back. she worked hard up until the day she gave birth. it's considered that it will make the birth easier. where i'm from, when a woman feels the pangs of labor one morning, she takes a long walk. in a rocky pasture somewhere, she squats, pushes out pink squealing flesh from the flesh of her sex. she goes home and cleans up, cleans the baby. she's still got lunch set out on the table in time for the heat of mid-day. i would come in from playing outside all day when i was small, or from watching sheep when i was a bit bigger, and there'd be a new baby.

at the time when You and i left for Fes, the new baby was a girl. she was going to be called Hadoun.

my family could not spare a sheep to sacrifice, and they would have to kill a turkey for the naming of the baby. my grandmother had been dead for a year or two.

You never learned to speak. even now You don't speak. the others in our household had always harbored suspicion of You—You were something supernatural, something unexplained, and now perhaps the hidden cause of our trouble. there was growing resentment of You, another mouth to feed.

and Sheep, You know i was too big for that place. God meant me for a life it couldn't provide me, i know it. the world that creates you can't always sustain you. i couldn't always explain it but for my whole childhood i could feel a pounding in me, so urgent i sometimes couldn't sleep. in the dawn of Hadoun's naming ceremony—i was fifteen or sixteen—You and i walked to a neighboring village. i hid You in the back of a truck piled with rugs and climbed in after You, and we rode into the rising day.

years past that, years of learning this city's labyrinthine secrets, and i end up trapped in a cold room, spinning the myth of myself to Rachid—while i feel my blood surging, the same surge that took me out of the desert to Fes.

2

I know my parents felt something pulsing in them, that pulled them out of their country. me too, i felt something. i felt pulled up and down through the body of New York City, i felt pulled out of my bed at night. i swear. i was drawn by this music, by the bodies swaying on corners and the glitter of the chains that swayed from their necks.

i've left my city for my parents' city now. i brought two suitcases to Fes, one full of clothes and one full of records—Eric B. and Rakim, Afrika Bambataa, Curtis Blow, the Furious Five, the Boogie Boys, T La Rock, Red Alert, the Treacherous Three, Doug E. Fresh, Whodini...because for everything i've been told about this place i'm supposed to come from, i know that it is not my home. i want to be able to put a record on and close my eyes and just be in a basement in the Bronx, and try to hear the legs shuffling over a piece of cardboard on the floor, and try to imagine myself in the crowd that circles the breakdancer, belonging. i want You to use your hands like this to draw a record from its sleeve. and i want You to place it on the turntable, find the central hole where the metal spike goes. i want You to gently coax the needle from its holder and pull it across the air above the record, and i want you to stop the needle right here, right in this groove. i want You to lower the needle, and i want You to listen. because i know there is something for You there.

Fes is a restless city and a city of high tempers. it's about ready to buckle under the weight of itself. and where my Brooklyn was a place of fire escapes against brick buildings in endless repetition, ancient Fes is a place where you can sit on a terrace and your eyes can skip from flat rooftop to flat rooftop, your mind escaping like a deft thief until it reaches the wall of the old city and shimmies down.

the bebs of Fes—the gates to the city—like giant keyholes. when i first came my cousin Rachid was in jail, a fact that i relished. it was so far from the image i'd had of him. i had only visited my parents' city once before in my life, when i was too small to remember. a few times a year my parents called his and passed the phone around the house, and i heard that Rachid's voice had grown a bit since last time, but that it was still a serious voice and still sounded disappointed to be speaking with me. i wondered what he would rather be doing. maybe kicking a soccer ball with the other boys in his neighborhood, crying out impassioned when his team made a goal in an overturned trash can? more likely, he wished he was torturing himself behind the pages of some book.

i spent my first week in Fes waiting in Rachid's house. Khalti Miriam, his mother, kept my glass of hot mint tea everlastingly replenished. we watched TV for hours and discussed the finer plot points of her favorite Egyptian soap opera like scholars. in the secret of nighttime, i smoked the butts of my uncle's spliffs from ashtrays around the house. in the mornings i sat on the roof with the maid and watched her beat rugs to the wind, and watched the sun caught in the dust that flew from them, watched the thousands of rows of laundry flapping above the city from its layers of terraced roofs. i imagined my name grafittied across the city in sacred calligraphy, *Aisha Aisha lives, lives Aisha lives lives*, my name Alive.

in that week i started to collect in myself the house's heavy habit of longing. we waited for cousin Rachid, the golden son, who was overheard saying the wrong thing about the wrong people and got arrested for it. the ceiling of the house is open to heaven, the better for our prayers to slip up into the sky. a deep dust coats its high wood rafters. it is full of heavy wool tapestries and silver teaware tarnished by generations.

my parents sent me back to their country because i was bad, and they sent me because i am their failed American dream. i could tell You about it, except that ever since cousin Rachid brought me to You i want so much for You to love me, and sitting to play music with You makes me feel alive, like my name should make me feel, like i haven't felt in so long.

When i finally arrived home from prison the sun was beginning to go down. the front door to my family's house is off of an inconspicuous alleyway. i knocked. from behind the door: 'shkoun?' it was the voice of Layla, who had been my nursemaid when i was small and helped us now in the kitchen. as a child not much bigger than me, she had raised me. strange how, with time, we find ourselves towering over the heroes of our youth.

'a relative,' i called back, my voice weak. Layla flung open the door, flung her arms around me. i entered. i had returned to my childhood home, its centuries-old carved wood, its smell of dust-gathered wool, its echoes. my mother sat in the salon with many other people. my mind felt too tired to try to recognize them all, but among them was my cousin Aisha from America, the daughter of my mother's sister. i kissed my mother's hand. she covered her mouth with the other hand, and her eyes began to fill with water. she's always been theatrical. i had hoped to avoid that.

the night i was snatched off the street and pushed, struggling, into prison, i thought that when everything was over—as it would be soon, i clung to my faith in that—i would return to classes and quietly resume my life. but what can we do when time passes, and transforms one truth into another? we're helpless. there are things i want so much to forget now. it is the first time in my life i have had in me such an urge to forget. i want my memory clean. we can never go backwards. it's always been an obvious fact, but now its simplicity falls away for me, and i recognize that the truth underneath it is sad. with a glass of tea before me and the room around me static-charged with the voices of others, i fall still and retreat into myself: i am torn between wanting to forget, and feeling pulled still further towards an irreversible future that can't help but to take where i've been with me.

it should be a natural skill for me, forgetting. we are so artful at manipulating the past. in our hands history is pliant, what has been done can be removed from the record of time, what has passed can live again.

i know people can be erased. we can disappear, evaporate, rise like smoke into the sky. i think of the rebel Ben Barka, his broken body dissolved in a vat of acid. the living rumor of him shattered—

we can be made to have never existed.

likewise, the life that faded centuries ago can be made to appear as though it never vanished, as though it is still something so real that you can eat and drink it—though it slips through you, and leaves no trace of nourishment in your body.

earlier that day, my first day back out into the city, i had waited for the feeling of being alive again to overtake me. i thought of flinging my arms out into it, but didn't want to look foolish.

so for whatever reason, no feeling of freedom came. Fes seemed at first to be as it always was, as it always has been, as it always will be, but betraying the corruption of its age. it is grey, its walls threaten to crumble. the flat clustered houses in the medina lean lopsided against one another. i watched two men fight on the street, until they were separated by a stranger. no, there was a new suspense in the air of my city, a hunger. i can't say whether i could feel this hunger because it was new, or because the experience of prison had endowed me with a new capacity to identify with the hungry.

a police officer had guided me out of the cell, put his arm paternalistically around my shoulders. he told me that they try their best to avoid these kinds of misunderstandings, that good sons of Fes like me have no business in places like this. smiling at him, i reached for the key to Aziz's apartment in my pocket, closed my fingers around it and remembered the mission he had given me, thought of You.

on my walk home, i had turned onto a crushingly narrow side street, one that i have walked hundreds of times. since i was small i have had the irrational fear that its rough concrete sides will close in on me, and i can never avoid scraping an arm against one of them. this time a cat with green eyes sat in the middle of my path and stared into me, then turned and took off in front of me on feather-light paws. i wandered out of my way to follow it, and because i had been looking down i nearly collided with a friend from university, Hamid. he greeted me with a sound hug, and welcomed me back, as the noon call to prayer sounded from a minaret above us. he asked me to lunch with his family, and i followed him to his house.

there we all dipped our bread into the same dish, a chicken tagine. his mother, gap-toothed and ample-bosomed, beamed at me the whole meal, pushing the nicest portions of meat towards me. after the meal she deftly sliced and portioned a sweet yellow melon, eating pieces herself as she went. i leaned back. i put my hands on my belly, satisfied, and praised God. i rinsed my hands and face with water, and Hamid walked me out through the alleyways that lead from his door.

'who do you think turned you in?,' he asked, as we stood under a dark, cool archway. i shrugged my shoulders and told him i didn't. didn't think about it.

'you think it was someone who wanted revenge?,' he asked. i said i didn't know. i told him i figured it was just word of mouth, somebody told somebody who told somebody who cared. Fes is a mirror. i shrugged again, and told him i'd race him to the top of Talaa Kabira. we ran breathless uphill. we dodged a donkey laden with Coca

Cola bottles that clinked chime-like to the pace of its feet, and a boy who walked with bare feet and a sack of grain on his head. Hamid got to the top a little before me. winded, i patted his arm. i told him, 'i used to think that I could conquer Fes, but Fes always won. Fes always wins. and Fes is always right, even when it's wrong—like your parents.'

only my parents will die one day, and Fes is eternal.

there at the top of that hill, looking down the muddy street's bottomless slope, i decided that i would try to avoid my friends from university, and that i would not return to school. i had been studying law, not only because my mother thought there should be a lawyer in our family, but because i had been obsessed with unfairness. i was ranked second in my class. but there are no jobs for us, when we leave school. and i've grown so tired of chasing ideas. *Chasing sleep, laying on the sofa in a salon upstairs, i begin to think of the sound of the train back home, and it soothes me, to hear the metal rushing against itself again and feel that i'm tunneling below the city—another city, far away—with hundreds of strangers.* with Bone i had become almost nomadic. we used to ride the train from one end to the other, then back again, sometimes all day. he had named himself. when i would walk with him he used to point out his name, splattered in beautiful neons against some wall. his name would be hiding around a corner, or i'd look up when i waited for the L and it would light the train alive like a dragon, come snaking past.

Bone lived the most interesting life of anyone i'd known yet. he was among the throng of boys crawling through subway tunnels in earliest morning, like cockroaches through sewers—risking the safety of their bodies for it. dropping from the third-story windows of family apartments in darkness, sneakers slapping the ground, to join the city-wide scramble to cover every last piece of wall with text. stirred from their sleep by the urge to write their names, calligraphied, letters twisting into one another, bloated beyond recognition and falling into each other. these boys over whose shoulders i'd peek in class, to see them stylizing their new names on scraps of paper. the blank surface compelled them, whether wall or toilet stall or geometry notebook.

Bone would nod in recognition on the street at skinny boys with tell-tale fingers stained with paint, tell-tale t-shirts ruined, sacrificed to creeping blotches of it. kids twelve years old sometimes, and grown men. walking with him, it seemed the walls were speaking a language, that he must have for sure had a code for. he knew which neighborhood each writer was from. he would show me where one writer had written over another, to stake his claim. how beautiful, to write your name on a city. i wrote his name on my body in thick magic marker. because i wanted to feel claimed by him, see? as though i, like the ugly city, might be redeemed by it. i traced over it again in the morning, you know? morning after morning. even after we were quits i'd find myself tracing his name with a fingernail on my skin. then it was like his name came to haunt me, haunted even my own fingertips. everywhere i'd go, i'd see his name, on a wall in lower Manhattan, trampled by a bearded Hassid on a sidewalk by my house. before i met him i used to hang out with a friend from school, Wanda. her mom was a nurse who worked the night shift at a hospital nearby. she wore slippers covered in plastic and had deep purple bags under her eyes. Wanda was this b-girl and she used to know how to do a dance she called the Red Jerk. it was great, You'd have to see it. we'd go upstairs to her room at night, and her mom would call up when she left. then me and Wanda would get dressed to go out. she had a purple eye shadow she let me borrow. i'd hold a mirror to paint my eyes, sitting on the edge of the bathtub while the hot comb heated. as it grew hotter it released the smell of the burning hot oil stuck between its teeth. i kept motionless while Wanda slid the comb through, smoke rising from my head, my naps transformed as if by alchemy into something limp and compliant. 'you kinda light to have hair so kinky,' Wanda said to me from above my head, 'but there, you cute now'—using a scrunchie and greasing everything to one side.

i wore these polka dot tights with blue glitter on them with my high-top Chucks. me and Wanda rode the train for hours into the South Bronx and we'd find ourselves in a basement somewhere, and there would be someone spinning a fantastic beat, and the bass would wedge itself somewhere between my heart and my belly, grab me and keep pumping. and when she felt like it, had a few drinks in her or had been bobbing her head in a corner too long until the music gathered in her too and started to play with her limbs—Wanda would set herself whirling out into the floor, and she could battle even the dudes. i would watch. yeah, and one night we heard a gunfight blocks away, and the whole party grew hushed. it was like something from a dream i'd had—i don't know why anybody else stopped and grew still, but for me it was because i had started to dream of guns, to wonder about them, although the only ones i'd ever seen were dangling from the belts of police officers. and one night i met Bone, the first boy to tell me i was pretty. i was the only one still sitting still for many moments after the sound of gunfire had faded. the party began to resume around me and the chatter of those we were gathered with washed over me but i couldn't move. eventually someone nudged my shoulder and i forced a smile to let them know i was okay. i chose to let myself get carried away by the beat again.

Wanda was one of few friends i'd had. now You, but what are You? why don't You speak? it's like You're still learning to be human; eyes apologetic, posture sloped, hoping that the shape of You fits well enough into a room. yeah, and this is what draws me to You, what lodges itself in me—because maybe i'm only pretending to be human too, hoping that no one can see through my act. and how often i've felt as i think you feel: slouching at the margins, wishing i possessed an ounce of that one intangible thing that could make me belong. i want to put a voice into your body.

I didn't sleep well, my first night back at my parents' house. i haven't slept well in a long while. in prison i tried at first to sleep as often as i could, in an effort to make the time pass more quickly. but there came a point when i couldn't satisfy myself, couldn't sleep enough to feel replenished. i'd wake up as tired as i was before. and then i grew unable to shut my eyes at all. suspended in a sleepless limbo, i was sluggish and inert, and powerless to call my faculties back to me.

now, even safe at home, i lay awake until dawn. i can't recall what thoughts i'd drawn to myself to keep me company, but that's just as well. i want to abandon the world of ideas. maybe You can teach me.

i waited for the sun to find a settled place in the sky before i crept from bed. i hoped to make a quick exit from the house without disturbing anyone. only a servant, Abdelkarim, was awake, and i could hear him moving things around in an upstairs room. i stood and leaned against a counter in the kitchen to eat a quick breakfast before i left, bread and some processed cheese and powdered coffee.

Aziz's house was on the other side of the medina from ours.

on the way i was struck by the face of one beggar, a woman who did not meet my eyes when i searched for hers, and i dropped two coins into her open hands. i find myself touched more easily by beggars lately. i find myself identifying with my city in a new way, because i realize that all of us here share the same condition: that we are all fallen, that we've all had our dignity

28

robbed from us, that we are all neglected by the only powers we can think to turn to. i became lost in the smell of fresh coriander from the vegetable souk. i went to buy a few things.

i had recorded Aziz's precise directions to his apartment on the back of a brown piece of cardboard. twisting down an alleyway, walking up the stairs, i found his door. i tried to use my key, but found that the lock had been broken. i pushed the door open— inside i am shocked to find the same beggar i had given alms to earlier, sitting on a banquette, holding a bunch of mint leaves and eating from it, raw: it's You.

You run to a corner, shaking, so frightened that i can almost hear your heart beat from across the room. i feel like an intruder. i don't even dare to speak to You, because i worry that a word would disturb you even further.

i had only been asked to make sure that You were alive, and to provide You with what seemed necessary to keep You that way. i hadn't been asked to be your friend, had i? i decided that i would give myself a tour, examine the set-up. this way i could be clear about what you needed.

the apartment is one room, where there is a space for cooking and a space with a banquette for reclining. i ascend the stairs that lead to the roof, from where the medina below stretches and yawns like a cat. this roof looks over the open roof of the mosque next door, and i watch the men below put on their shoes after prayer and go back into the world. on the roof i find the toilet, a little closet with a hole in the ground. i go back down into the room.

listening to Aziz talk about himself gave me the impression that he lived like a king, that years of trading hashish had made him the lord of Fes. but i have never entered a simpler or humbler home. it occurs to me just now that homes like this are hidden all over my city—little holes where people are making lives for themselves, corners and cubbies probably even on the street where i grew up. there is so much i don't know about the place where i have lived my whole life, the city i have hardly ever left. there is one cupboard in the room. i open it to inspect its contents: three plates, a box of tea, a pile of oranges, one of which rolls onto the floor. it's covered in green and white mold, so i throw it out the window.

i cough into my glasses to clean them, to get the clearest impression of this place. in this moment a memory comes to me, of getting my first pair of glasses when i was very small. i hadn't even noticed the change in my eyesight, but when my teacher had pointed to a small enough letter at a far enough distance, i couldn't read it. my parents insisted that i be taken to the eye doctor. my legs dangled from the big leather chair where i sat, while a monstrous machine with thousands of pieces of clicking glass inside was pushed onto my face to inspect me. when i walked from that dark room, i picked out a bright blue frame, the one i liked better than any of the others that were available for me to choose.

i returned from the doctor's and came into my classroom as the room lay in shadow. the windows were covered and the other students lay napping on mats on the floor. my teacher told me how nice i looked in my new glasses. but i felt different, removed. now there was a window between me and the world. now i watched what went on around me from behind glass. at that age, i myself had been unconcerned by my vision, and i had not been aware that it was inadequate. i didn't feel defective. i felt like myself. if my eyes were becoming bad, it was something that was occurring beneath my own awareness.

i remember wondering then at the secret life of the body, the hidden life of the very flesh we inhabit. my city is like that.

and You are one of its secrets. i suppose You have sustained yourself by begging since Aziz has been gone.

since i've been here You haven't moved from your corner, and it frustrates me, that You won't let me close to You. i don't want to cause You anymore distress, so i leave the bread, olives, and fruit i brought with me in the cupboard. then i leave, closing the door carefully. i walk home.

that evening after our dinner—slow roasted lamb with prunes—i sit with my father in his salon on the first floor, our legs crossed, and smoke kif with him from his long pipe. he tells me that he would like to take me to lunch soon, to celebrate my return. we talk about the rising price of bread, a conversation so popular that you can hear it in every café these days, and in most homes. 'i have always been certain that i will eat,' my father is saying, 'but i suppose even that is changing.' my father is as prone to melancholy as my mother is to melodrama. he has a way of drawing a fact out until it's long and mournful. still, it's true that time has taken a lot from our family. it won't stop until we have nothing, are reduced to ashes. that's the truth, isn't it? that we all become erased, in the end? 'how long can we fight it?,' i ask my father—'it,' that thing that is always winning.

smoke circles above our heads, a raincloud full of the electric static of thought, and we can hear my cousin play her music loudly upstairs. everything she does is to remind us that she's not one of us, or perhaps to remind herself. the music she's brought with her is jagged, full of metal, traffic, electricity. it does strange things to my ears. i had been trying to avoid Aisha since i got home today. she is curious about me, and seems to want something of me that i can't give. she sat in the room with me as i unpacked some books, 'what's jail like?,' she asked me. 'quiet,' –my response was quick.

now she breaks my train of thought with that noise. my father had fallen asleep on himself and i had begun to think about You. You are winning the fight, i think, while the strategies of so many others fail. a question Aziz had posed aloud as i sat with him begins to unfurl, and, like the smoke above us, to unravel into nothing : the question how You survived those two months without him.

You broke the lock and went out into the world, then. You begged. You sustained yourself off of nothing. You must have some kind of magic. You survive. i try to imagine an origin for You, the circumstance that created You: some scared young mother in the south abandoning her infant against a rock in the cruel wilderness, and the infant's refusal to die, preferring instead to barter humanity for survival among a passing flock of sheep.

an electric pounding forces itself downstairs from one of Aisha's records and it occurs to me that perhaps if i take her to You, it will become easier for me to approach You myself. she is a girl, firstly. she annoys me, but it's because she's so relentlessly open with herself. i know she will make an easy friend for You, and i think she may be able to calm You, to slowly open You.

3

Me and a beggar have only one thing in common: that we both profit from people's need to escape their guilt. i'll give begging its due credit as its own profession: you take your particular physical affliction—your twisted limb, your palsy, your gaping wound—and parade it in the streets with your hand out. if you're an unmarried woman, i know a few neighborhoods where you can rent a child out; hug it to yourself, learn to look into the eyes of passerby with an intensity not to be mistaken for boldness.

i despise a beggar, though. me and You came up from nothing and we never had to ask for nothing we didn't deserve. when i first came to this city i had no name, no training, no trade. i was taking You with me everywhere, refused to leave You. Fes, the medieval city, crushed in on us from all sides. it stole the light of day, it cast a constant shadow even over an afternoon's brilliance.

we had rolled off the truck both smelling like wool. it was nighttime and suddenly we were in the city for the first time. Fes' walls stood stark against the sky and we found ourselves peering up at them, feeling like tiny insects. the walls made me think of giant anthills— masses of dust. they seemed on the verge of collapsing into enormous heaps of sand. later i learned that the city had been a fortress, had been impenetrable. now it was a skeletal homage to its former self, and it was wide open. maybe that's why i caught the feeling of being a soldier, of being an ancient enemy of the city, of sneaking up on it stealthy while it slept, even though i was just a boy, and You were keeping stride next to me: because maybe i wasn't the first boy soldier who'd tried to slip into Fes and maybe, in the eyes of a city like Fes with its thousands of people and thousands of years—even You weren't the first of your kind.

You and i walked; it was the only thing i could think to do. i had never seen a city before, not really, not unless i thought of the dusty towns i'd peeked at from beneath the carpet that day as cities—a hanout each, a mosque each, and each with its obligatory sleepy café where men with no teeth drank coffee in plastic chairs and a pretty girl with fat hands was pouring tea in a perfect crystal arc that a bit of sun glinted through.

we walked up stone steps outside the city's walls—i took your hand. You were always trusting of me and i've tried to pay You back for it the best i can, to give You the best kind of life in return. the trust You've put in me has been a gift. with it, i became something —where in the desert i'd had to surrender myself to sleep in the heat of mid-day just to keep from being obliterated by the sun, and i felt steadily that i was nothing. me and my family, we were mankind, and for mankind we pressed against the steady facts that nature would erase us as individuals, each in our turn, and it barely mattered what our names were, and it barely mattered who we thought we were—it mattered that we lived. You and i walked past what i now know to be the tombs of kings, white graves, blue in the starlight, and they inspired a silence in us. the whole city was sleeping, and when Fes sleeps it's a monument to solitude—after all these years, it still makes me want to bow my own head not in sleep but in awe. we walked past the iron fence of a nice hotel whose open palm fronds were rustling in the wind. gates closed to us, but i squinted my eye so i could see past to the hotel's glimmering starry swimming pool, and further into its tall windows lit like portraits—inside a lady in a red-striped uniform with a pristine white cloth tied over her head pushed a mop over the floors, floors that shone like God's heaven, or something else forbidden to people like us.

up and up the old stone steps until we came to a broken stone wall, and leaned together against it. what was

this city that even muted the stars? it was a power i wanted
a piece of. The very night before, the stars in the sky above
me had been clustered uncountably; but in the sky over
Fes stars were spaced far apart, no more than fifty of them.

dizzy under this new kind of starlight we fell
asleep against the wall, and we woke to the blinding sun
between our eyelashes. we rose, and went back down the
stone stairs, back past the hotel and its immaculate glass
windows that in daylight glared the world outside back at
itself, the white medina down the hill now shining, and all
i could think, passing those clean windows, was that they
wanted to be shattered—in a vision i saw them so, in jagged
pieces reflecting the brilliant city in a thousand directions.

what i couldn't have realized in those first moments
in Fes—as my boyhood was shaking off me like the grains of
red sand i'd carried from home in the fibers of my clothing—
was that the hallucinogenic heat of the desert was also rising
off of me, shuddering off of me to leave me and never return.
Fes gave fewer stars and it surrendered fewer of its dream-
visions—until the world came to settle around me and to
fix itself, no longer something that wavered and warped, a
mirage on the horizon, the insect you thought you saw but
you didn't see in the dust at your feet, the voice you thought
you heard but didn't hear on the wind. not even now in
the cold clarity of this jail, all of my senses peaked, do the
simple visions of the desert return to me, not even here
does time morph into that slow syrup that the unbearable
sun used to melt it to when i was a kid. sometimes i still
don't know whether it was the loss of my childhood or the
loss of the desert—maybe it was only the reverberating
aftershock of being hit with all Fes' force, a shock that
echoes between your bones as long as you live to survive it.
if i'd arrived in Fes by myself, my future there might have
taken a different course—maybe i would have taken up

with a pack of boys my own age, followed them, foraged with them, fought with them when it got so cold that i needed to see someone's blood to remind myself there was still life under the earth and under the skin.

but i had You. whatever You were, You were not a boy, and i knew that world—scrambling through the city at night like cockroaches—was not for You. if i was to live in that kind of world myself, i'd need to find You shelter from it.

so that day i found us our first home in Fes, a piece of cardboard in the Mellah, slanted against a corner in a dead-end derb. i told You to stay there, that the city was dangerous for You, and You obeyed me. i spoke to my first Fessi that day, a man who started a conversation with me on the street, whose language i couldn't understand. he laughed at the confusion on my face, and called me a name—i understood only the contempt behind it, not the word. i would have to learn the tongue of the city. and that day i chose a new name for myself, an Arab name for the Arab city. without a voice, i knew you would never reveal my origins.

in the days that we lived there i used to slip through the medina around lunchtime (when everybody was drowsy of asleep, fat-bellied, unfocused) to steal a loaf of bread and some oranges. i'd take it back to You—peel your orange for You and place each section into the palm of your hand, and with each piece of fruit i'd tell another story about what had happened that day. i don't know my exact age even now, but i think i was fifteen or sixteen at that time. it was spring, so we were lucky. i had never experienced winter yet in my life. after i had, springtime always urged me to forget it, that cold in my bones—and it always recalled our arrival in the city, for me, the feeling of being free and loose in the world and the sense of power and responsibility You gave me. we came to Fes in the months before the sun begins to bear on you too hard, to press the juice out of you until you want to curse it. we fooled ourselves for a while, in the sun's mercy. before that spring was over, i had abandoned stealing, and moved on to other things. it was because i'd nearly gotten caught one day. the man at the shop had turned from me when i swiped a loaf, but he turned back again too soon. i had started to ease away with the bread in my hand. he saw me. embarrassed, i walked back to him. i smiled at him, asked how much, though i knew that the price wouldn't matter. there was not a coin in my pockets—there never had been, and i had never handled money in my whole life up to that point. i placed the bread back at the top of the stack, where it was illuminated by a single hanging light bulb. from the back of the shop, the king's portrait stared at me disapprovingly. i had built a tin lean-to for us and we had been living there for about a week, in an abandoned garden hidden deep in Geurniz. i didn't want to alert anyone to our presence, so i was afraid to plant much in the soil yet, though we sometimes ate the thin wild onions that we found growing there. but this was the second day in a row that i came home to You with nothing substantial to put into our bodies, and it would be the second night in a row we slept with our stomachs grinding in on themselves. i braced myself for the look of disappointment on your face, as you rose from your place and saw that i had nothing for You.

i'd thrown up a clear plastic tarp over the walls as our ceiling. the day's last light came trickling in like dirty water. You rose from the dust floor when i entered, looking concerned. i thought You must be able to sense that i had failed You again that day. but You were turning to look at the dust on the floor where you had been sitting, still impressed with your body. parts of the earth clumped together there with dark blood, your blood. You were confused and terrified. i had nothing to offer You.

i found the woman who begged outside a mosque nearby to show you what to do about woman-things.i felt severed from You. i knew it was inevitable that You would betray me, and continue to betray me. You were not sexless.

Sheepinawoman'sbody,abodythatwouldalwaysbetray You—icouldnotsaveYou,fromtheconsequencesofyourbody.

Winter was nothing to me, before i came to Fes. we bundle ourselves up where i come from. outside we walk briskly, so quick that we shield ourselves from the warmth of human contact, quick enough to feel our blood fill with hot rage against the cold. inside our homes there's the heat of the radiator and the familiar smell it makes as it burns the air. when the snow gets so thick your boots can't cut through it, so thick it cuts your eyes as it falls slanted from heaven—you go inside, and there you're safe. but here in Fes you can't escape the chill of winter. the houses in the medina aren't heated, and when i wake up in my aunt's house, peeking out from under two wool blankets, i can see my own breath suspended in the air above my bed.

the day i met You i lay in bed all morning, watching a line of ants crawl over the zellige pattern on the floor, animated dots that followed the zig-zag grooves between the diamond tiles. i haven't left Rachid's house much since i've been here. once i went to the hammam with Khalti. then another night i went out with her and her friends, all wearing jellaba and linking arms, me on the end of the line, in jeans. we made a tour out of visiting people that night, ate pastries and sipped hot coffee in strange salons. i felt like a curiosity. 'this is Aisha from America,' my aunt said, and the women in the salon raised their eyebrows. as one person, they all said 'ah,' like they knew something about me that i didn't.

my cousin Rachid came into the stale house like a cool breath. he had never before seemed like someone that i might enjoy hanging out with, but now he's been in trouble with the law. i know he must have secrets. he must have something dangerous coiled inside him. he found me a few nights ago in the salon upstairs where i keep my things. i had been playing Boogie Down Productions loud enough that the music filled a space inside my head, and he had reached to turn it down so that i could hear him. he said, 'tomorrow, prepare yourself like you're going to meet a new friend.'

typical of him, he was being deliberately mysterious. but i was still excited and eager to follow him, to see what he was about. on the way to your house the next afternoon he said that You were the sister of a drug dealer he had become friends with in prison and that he'd been asked to take care of You. cousin Rachid, who by my brief impression seemed pretty boring, is friends with criminals now—i love it.

'she doesn't speak,' Rachid said. so i thought to heft Khalti's record player and one of my records under one arm and we wove through the medina, me and Rachid, past vendors with electronics spread out on the ground. we walked for a while behind a man who held two live bound roosters by the feet, and in the flap of their wings was a revelation that it would rain soon. we were passing a square filled with music from the hammers of craftsmen against bronze kettles. we wound through Fes' insides, until we came to an open door at the end of an alley, and walked up a dark staircase, and pushed open the entrance to your apartment, and found You. your body tensed when You saw Rachid, but i sat next to You, and took your hand, felt your fingers with my thumb. You became calm.

'what is she eating?,' i asked Rachid. if we were to look after You, i guessed, we should feed You.

'i think she eats anything. she eats things raw, i think, but i left her some bread and some olives.'

then You rose, and Rachid and i watched to see what You would do. your hands shook and i felt that You must be nervous under our gazes, but You went to the corner where there was a tank of butane for cooking. still shaking, but steadying yourself, You took a match, lit a flame, and put on a pot of boiling water. You served me and Rachid hot tea, with lots of sugar but without mint. we blessed and thanked You, and then You smiled. a beautiful smile. 'but doesn't she have a real name?,' i asked Rachid.

'Aziz just called her Sheep. i don't know if she was given one. she was found as a small child.'

'so she doesn't have a mama?'

'somewhere we all have a mama, but that's all i know,' Rachid said. he was getting annoyed with me. on my fingers i counted the facts as i mouthed them silently: *no name, no voice, no mother.* i smiled at You and tried to catch your eye.

there was something animal about You. and though all the muscles of your body seemed tensed in alarm at our presence, beneath this—beneath the rippling skin, the body's readiness to flee in a second—was something deeply unafraid, in You. as though your apparent fear was only to protect You, to stave off any predatory advance.

Rachid went to the roof to watch the sun go down. that was when i showed You how to play the record i had brought. the music struck You and You moved your shoulders, narrowed your eyes in concentration. i noticed the ring of dirt at the back of your neck, and saw that your hair was dirty.

i want you to be cleaner than you've ever been. today i asked Rachid to let me take You to the hammam. in the evening i take a bag with things for the bath in it, and come to see You. You are lying on the sofa, remembering something. You look up, and your eyes greet me. the blind rooster your neighbors keep on their roof, ignorant of the hour, wails in search of the sun. 'we're going to the hammam,' i tell You, and You lean close to me, interested in the idea. i take You by the hand and lead You down the stairs. we are outside. You seem to thrill with this freedom, and as your eyes search the crowd, imagining the lives of these strangers, it seems to me that You are also imagining possible escape routes. there's a man on your street who has a tiny stall, not wide enough for him to move his body from a fixed spot. he sells only buttons, thousands of colored buttons, and nothing else. i am unfamiliar with this neighborhood, so i ask him where there's a bath house nearby. looking up from his work—polishing a yellow button to fix it to a white shirt—he points across the street.

the back room of the hammam, the hottest and the darkest, is full of the dewey-skinned bodies of women of all ages and their children. there is a rich steam threaded with the smell of smoke from the wood furnace that heats the water. light comes from one lamp on the back wall, playing in the puddles on the floor; the room is soft and fuzzy at its edges. i clear a place for us in the front room, where the only other person is a wrinkled hajja, her white hair brightly hennaed with red. she asks me to wash her back. i am conscious of not having the seasoned back-scrubbing technique of a woman who's been to the hammam every week since she was born; but hajja is grateful for what i can give her, and she blesses my parents, and she wishes me many rewards in heaven.

then i scrub You, and the only sound in the room is the splash of water poured against your skin, echoed against the high, empty ceilings. i laugh and hear my laugh come back to me, bounced from the walls. i wash your hair three times. i scrub your body with the rough *kis* until dirt and even your own skin is sloughed off in fat grey slugs. i scrub myself hard too, and rinse the dirt from my body.

You're seized by deep relaxation. You heave a deep sigh, and your eyes become steamed and glassy with gratitude and peace. i know that You feel like a part of something. Rachid told me that You begged, while Aziz was gone—a position that placed You somewhere outside the humanity of those whose generosity You depended on. and i know that You have spent most of your time apart from that inside. i know, also, from the kind of nervous energy your legs seemed to carry as we'd walked, that they are yearning to run, and run.

is this your first time coming out into the world to come to a place where You belonged? is this the first time that You are part of the world's insides, warm and among others like You—beneath their clothes, equally naked and helpless?

i dry You with the blue towel i took from Khalti. You wear the clean pajamas i brought You under your worn, dull jellaba.

we think of the tiny life of the button man as we pass him on the way home.

My father took me to eat lunch at the nicest hotel in the city, Les Merinides. it stood on a hill that looked high above the old city. we wound in a taxi up through the ghettoes that line the mountain's edges where sleepy men hunched their shoulders as they walked with their canes and laundry flapped bright and defiant from every window—the patchwork flag of a new nation. as i'd never noticed before, i saw the poor that clamored up the hill, stopped from entering the bounds of the hotel by an unspoken, invisible boundary, like the electric fence i once saw yoke a friend's dog back with unseen hands when i visited his family's house in the new town.

the doors were opened for us and we walked through the lobby until we reached the garden terrace, where we were met with a breeze and the sound of a singing bird. in the garden just beyond a fence there were waving olive trees, the black fruit peeking from between the cool leaves, and there were palm trees with tendrils of ivy creeping up them. inside the hotel we only speak French, and only French is spoken to us. my father is a proud Fessi with a lilting, poetic accent to his speech, but when i hear him speak a foreigner's language i have trouble identifying his voice with the body that seems to be projecting it—his French is monotonous, like the language of a butler who doesn't dare impose his own humanity on the people he serves—like the language of the butler before us, who asks us what we'll eat: two bleeding steaks, that we stab at nervously to draw more blood.

my parents occupy our house like two great planets whose orbits never coincide. neither one leaves the house much. for my father this is a rare outing to mark the precious occasion of my return. without his kif for a few hours, he is more anxious than usual, fumbling with his fork and knife. looking at the top of his bald head from across the table, and listening to him talk about insignificant things in a stranger's tongue, his mood curiously agitated, he strikes me as a cripple. i have to eat faster, so fast that i know i'll have indigestion later, to smother the pity for him that wells in me suddenly. this is not where i want him. this weak old man is not my father, this man who remarks on the weather in the shaky words of his colonial schooling. i remember a time, maybe a week before i was arrested, when a neighbor visited our house, an old friend of his. it was the first time i felt a shame for his habit so sharply: his vision was glazed and he could barely make conversation. our friend was uneasy, and i explained to him that my father needed rest as i guided him out. in the sweet smells of this garden, white clouds above us like puffs of breath, i wonder who i have to become to allow him a fragile faith in his own strength. the task of becoming that person daunts me.

the next day i am walking, alone, on a hill from where i can see Beb Fetuah, on the very opposite side of the medina's perimeter as the hotel where i'd eaten lunch the day before. from there, i had looked out at the very winding road i walk along—kilometers away, automobiles twisting down it like shiny beetles. from the hilltops on the outer edges of the medina, you can look out across the whole of the old city. sometimes the view catches you by surprise.

with a book in my hand, i suddenly look up—it stops my heart. Fes sprawling white and dusty, its green minarets like little toy towers. i imagine the people moving in there, tiny. i hear the sound of a motorcycle come up at me and i try to picture it zipping down a small, infinite street. Fes reaching out of Mount Zalagh's valley with its fingers, gripping the sides of the valley to keep ahold of the turning world.

i'm reading a book about a family of seven in Egypt. before i can see even him i've run into my friend Hamid again—because if there's a principle that this city never fails to deviate from, it's that it will always lead you to the person you least want to see that day. by now everyone that i went to school with is probably aware that i've been released from jail. i don't even want to imagine what works of fantasy about my situation are being spun from their mouths and bantered between them. if the street cats in Fes have seven lives, we Fessis have at least three bodies: one that goes about our physical routine every day, one that only lives in our private dreams, and one that is only alive in the vast web of gossip that we all find ourselves unwittingly born into.

Hamid tells me that i must join him and some others at a café in Rcif. i know from the second he begins to ask that i will not be able to think of an excuse fast enough to decline his invitation. so in the end i follow him down the hill and back into the medina, which seems to be spread and waiting like the warm body of a woman. the café is one that is mostly patronized by men who sell the parts of automobiles, which Hamid chooses to frequent in strange homage to his father: an auto-mechanic who died with a black streak of engine oil on one cheek, consumed by a despair that had masqueraded as an anonymous disease. i had to come here once some years ago, to ask about a new muffler for an uncle's car.

Hamid and his friends have three tables at the back, cramped up against each other. one has a bottle of wine from Meknes under the table, and every now and then he sneaks a drop of it into his flat brown soda. stale cigarette smoke clouds the air, and a tape player in the corner sends out the whine of *rai*, Cheb Housni singing about a girl.

i smile at them uneasily. i don't always remember to be as polite as i've been taught to be, but somehow this congregation of young men my own age inspires me to shake hands around their circle, and to draw my own hand to my heart as i introduce myself.

'oh yes, we've heard of you,' says one, who i recognize as an economics major a year below me. i look to Hamid, whose gaze—like those of the others—seems fixed on me with some kind of pride or awe.

'i wish i'd known i would see you today,' Hamid says, 'so i could have invited Saiid to sit with us. he's so interested in getting to see you again.' Said was in the same program as me at school, and was ranked right below me—now, i guess, he has my spot in class. we had not been friends, but i can recall entering the same rooms as him now and then, and having the distinct impression that his eyes were on me, although if i searched for them they always seemed to have rested somewhere else.

the one drinking wine—whose name escapes me—offers me a sip, and i think about it, but decline. a soccer match roars from a television at the front of the café. it's the first time i've been back in a social setting like this since the night i was taken.

here i learn that a strike is being planned in a few days. Fes is forgotten, they say. they want to call attention to our hunger. they believe that if they shout loud enough they can be heard for hundreds of kilometers, maybe even across the world. they are asking that no one in the city work on that day, and they are holding a march through the whole city. i myself am learning to accept hunger as a fact. i consider that lesson part of what it means to become a man. after my experience in prison, i know hunger now, and i've known desire so tangible that it walks into a room where i sit, alone, and pulls up a chair next to me, and sighs at the same time as i do—so dear a friend that we know each other without words. 'what do you think?,' one called Mohammed asks me, 'we really respect your opinion.'

'the world is as it is,' i tell them. an old proverb comes to my mind, and i recite it for them: 'asking it to be anything more is like donkey's thinking.' 'it's disappointing to hear somebody like you, practically a hero, say something like that,' says the wine drinker.

'i'm not the hero you're looking for,' i tell them. 'everything that happened to me was a mistake.'

except coming to know You. now in this noisy, smoky room, i turn towards You in my mind, and a surge of peace comes to me.

Yesterday's lesson is shame: hshuma.

i'm upstairs on the terrace laying in the sun in a tank top and shorts and Khalti scolds me. 'the rooftop is not a private space. all the neighbors can see you. what kind of household will they think i run? hshuma.'

i squinted up at her. 'and also,' she's still saying, while pulling the towel i've brought from out under me, 'it's not good for your health. the longer you stay out in the sun during the day, the colder you'll be at night.'

still unsure about her logic, but compliant, i came downstairs whistling. Rachid reprimanded me: 'you can't do that in the house.'

'why?'

Rachid shrugs. 'hshuma. i'm not sure why, but why is not important.'

it probably has to do with calling spirits who might live in the house or something. at any rate i grab a piece of bread and tell him, 'well how should i know? i'm not from here.' 'forget that. if you were really a foreigner, it would be against the law for me to speak to you.'

'and we all know you don't break laws.'

'no,' said Rachid, buttering his bread with serious strokes of the knife, 'in fact, i don't.' today's lesson: my cousin is no hero.

'what did you do?,' i ask him. though i have learned that Rachid likes to think of himself as a secret, and am trying not to ask him many questions, i can't help becoming bold with him again—especially since i know we share a secret now in You.

'what did i do? what do you mean?'

'to get in jail, i mean, what did you do?'

'i didn't do anything,' Rachid tells me.

'ok.' i say. i pause to bite my lip, but i press him again: 'ok, so you're innocent?' Rachid meditates on the end of his cigarette and pushes at his glasses. he blows a sigh over his bottom lip, 'you don't know anything about this life.'

'so tell me.'

his eyes go up, as though he's searching hard for something at a spot above his own head, a small expression that makes me think of a dog in the impossible pursuit of its own tail. he tells me, 'i was just sitting in a café with some friends. we were looking at some pictures in a magazine, of the king in his bathingsuit on the beach in Agadir. i pointed at him and couldn't keep from laughing. i said to my friend, *the king has boobs.*'

'and then?'

'that's it. i was taken that evening, and when i got to jail they told me why. someone had heard me. perhaps they even hear me now.'

we have begun to escape Rachid's parents house regularly, to come see You. together Rachid and i prepare simple meals: omelets with potatoes in them, or the semolina porridge called smida, or the spiced white beans called loubia. when we make food i follow his directions—something i've never found easy to do, but which is beginning to come more naturally to me. it's clear that You aren't used to eating with others. You don't seem accustomed to dipping your hand into the same dish as us—sometimes it seems that You are shy of the food itself, but when i catch your eye and smile at You i can feel a courage gather in You. You usually make tea, and then You and i play some records. it's nice to know someone here who likes the same kind of music that i like. even if you've never heard something like this before it seems to please you. i could see from the first time that music brought something alive in you. it seemed to bring something like peace to your movements when you would sway, enraptured, to the beat. i could see the change come over you when the music began to play before my very eyes. i'm going to ask Rachid to find us a second turntable. i've noticed that You really like to play with the way the record spins, and i've heard You make some great sounds by scratching it. You have an instinct for drawing out patterns hidden in the music, for finding something new in a song i've heard hundreds of times. You caught this old r and b song by the skin at the back of its neck one time, and wrung it around—that's when the idea came to me that i'd train You as a DJ.

it's not like i'm an expert. back home i was more an expert at watching and dreaming than anything else. i always admired people who were good at doing things—it seemed to me that talent was something illusive and magical, something God hadn't found me worthy enough of. but sometimes i thought that if i stuck close enough to someone who had that magic, maybe some of the magic would stick to me.

in parks back home i had sometimes stood in

freestyle ciphers, the mass of young men circled around me, their words like rain to me, like water to my thirsty ears. i tried to be invisible, i hoped that no one noticed me, tiny between two anonymous sets of shoulders. i hoped no one could detect my girl-ness—my default, my deficiency, my powerlessness, my weakness—hoped no one could tell that i totally lacked the macho and the gusto that these dudes had, the force that propelled their voices from them. hoped no one resented the fact that i had nothing to contribute. over the park the sky would smooth into night, maroon and starless, washed out by the competing lights of the city. before Fes, i'd only seen stars at night once, on a class trip to Jersey in middle school, and i had called on movies i'd seen to give me an image i could compare them to. nights here, there's stars and sacred silence, and i remember something i'd forgotten before i was born.

in the night back home, i admired the ones like Wanda who could dance at parties. i admired the skilled hands that had flung color at Brooklyn's decrepit walls and made beauty of the city's decay—ashamed of my own hands when i sat at the table to eat with my parents, and embarrassed to think of bringing a friend home to dinner to watch us take food from the same plate, using bread and our fingers for silverware.

maybe i don't know anything myself. so what if i have no real skill of my own to give You? we're playing for ourselves. no one around here knows anything about real music. we're playing for no one.

Don't trust anyone in the city. even the one i'm sending to You—let him give You what You need, but don't trust him. people are wicked, and You're lucky to stand apart from us. maybe i'm talking to no one. i've made myself tired, repeating my own myth, a rhthym bouncing off itself. i speak to You and imagine that You hear me, but how can i know? i've withered, in these months, and it's all i can do to convince myself that i still exist somewhere—shining, glorious, heroic. if it is only in your memory, i want to know that i still exist, that i am not what i've become. i'll tell You one last time, as though the words echoed in my head are spoken aloud, as though i'm lulling You to sleep—and not alone, trying to spin myself into being. i want You remember how i rose, how i became powerful.

there was a time when i shone shoes. one day, after i'd come to realize that i couldn't feed us forever as a thief, i went up to another boy, a little younger than me, who was shining shoes at a café close to where You and i would one day have our apartment. i approached the shoe-shine boy as he leaned against a pole for a while, feet crossed at the ankles, absently beating his shoe-shine brush against the wooden footstool he carried—a sound that signaled to the men sipping steaming coffee at their tables that they could get their shoes shined, *dirham-dirham-dirham.*

i went up to this boy and i put two of my fingers between the footstool and the moving shoe-shine brush. when the brush hit me i cried out, and the boy noticed me. annoyed, he said, 'what's wrong with you?'

i put my hand to my mouth to suck my fingers and asked him where he got his brush and stool from.

he said he'd rent it out to me two days a week if i gave him half of what i made. so i accepted that. the day i took my coins to the *mul hanout* and bought us two loaves of bread from my earnings as a shoe-shine boy, it was the first time in my life i had handled money. first time i had ever exchanged money for goods. i thought it was a beautiful thing, the way coins clicked together cold in your hand. *mul hanout* gave me my change and i put one coin into my mouth, pressed it into my mouth's roof with my tongue. i tasted its metal, a taste like blood, and i felt its temperature melt to match my own. i took it out and placed it, hot and wet, in the center of my palm.

i went home to you and we ate bread with jam for

dinner, and for dessert i broke open a watermelon, red as flesh.

something about stooping at the feet of other men all day wasn't right to me, but i never let myself forget that i was better than them. you can't. the feel of metal money in my hands every day was teaching me something. by touch i could make out more than the cold faces of dead kings on a coin's flat face. i was learning a code, handling money— the code that was written in each coin's relative warmth and slime: the ghost of fingerprints, the hieroglyphics of exchange. each man before me had left the slick trail of his desires and it was something i could read with my own fingers. money, it seemed to me, was imperceptively imprinted with wanting, a recorded history of wanting. and listening to what coins had to tell me made me realize that even as i squatted on the ground to receive them, at that very moment the force of someone else's desire rested with me.

so i was a patient shoe-shiner. i held tight in me like a knot the conviction that even if i was selling my dignity at the shoes of people who regarded me as little more than something to be stepped on, despite all this i was the one who profited from our exchange. i could save a few coins in a soda can and still feed us. then i could take the coins to a shop owner and see them transfigured into paper. i started to buy cartons of French cigarettes so that i could sell single ones from corners. it meant i was gone from You more often. i never demanded anything of You, but You became a competent housekeeper in time. on your own, You saw that need and filled it. your head began to fill. i noticed You begin to order your day, place one task in your mind after another, build a plan for yourself and execute it: first sweep the floor, then go outside to enjoy the sun, then draw pictures in the dirt with your finger, then come inside to launder some clothes.

You started to have tea ready for me when i came home. i never asked these things of You but perhaps You were beginning to understand how grateful to me You should be, and how much You owed me. i hope You still remember. i gave You everything. i gave You all my life, so You could make it yours.

then don't wonder why i made the choices that followed. it wasn't because i was myself an addict. though i made my living in the field of addiction, i hate addicts. sometimes in order to maintain that hatred i roll it around inside me until it's a tight ball, until it makes me want to spit— until i do spit, and watch my spittle simmering on the ground. people like me and You, who come from nothing, understand how not to want anything. to survive the lonely horrors of the night into the next day, to survive the heat of the sun into cool night—that's a gift. we never took it as a guarantee. when i came to Fes and saw people who had so much still wanting, it made me laugh. and it made me want to master them.

i couldn't shine shoes and peddle loose cigarettes forever. i needed to be at the center of desire. my blood was fierce for it. i was tired of being looked at like a pitiful stray cat by the people i took my money from. i wanted men to look at me with the full conviction of their desire. when someone looks at you from that place somewhere beyond their own humanity, that world where their own bodies go about their secrets beneath the whims of the mind, that place where we are no more than animals—when someone looks at you from there, and you stare back at them, you can capture a part of them. this is the closest i will ever be to love: looking after the animal inside someone else. nothing else is essential, nothing else is important to me. most of the time i feel far from other men, but when i meet them at the place where they meet their own humanity, i feel alive.

i used to follow the man who sold hashish in our neighborhood. he kept his graying hair in a long braid down his back. once in a private moment in the dark of the hole where he lived, when we had become familiar with each other and he let me call him Uncle, i saw him unwind it, carefully brush it before a mirror, and rebraid it with the tender concentration of all his vanity. he walked jauntily, speaking to everyone he met.

i asked to run errands for him. i told him if he needed anything, i could help him. he asked me to clean his house— to remove the covers from the sofas and air them out, to throw water over the floor and sweep it into a drain in his floor. he started to ask me to bring him vegetables, fresh coriander and mint. after some months, when he had eyed me well enough, he asked me to run a package of kif to a nice old house in Rcif. it was then that i began to have the courage to ask how i could start to get more work like that—what i would have to do to be like him. 'you don't want to be like me,' he said, 'i'm old.' but the next week he sent me in an old taxi that coughed fumes into its own interior. we went up through the hills into the magical green region of Katema, where he received his supplies. i went with the man Uncle had told me to meet into forests of kif where women stooped to pick the crop under a sweeping sky, their heads wrapped in old rags.

the air there was peaceful and to breathe it felt healthy. it was the first time in the year since i'd left my own village that i'd been so far from Fes' stink and chaos. i ate a warm vegetable stew with the taxi driver and slept under the stars before we came back into the city. i had taken extra money with me, everything that was in the soda can in our house. i bought the kilos of hashish for Uncle, but i also bought a kilo for myself. when i returned to Fes, i was able to offer some of his customers the same quality for half the price. i built my own trust with Uncle's clients—while i continued to sit with him in his own house sometimes, and eat from the same dish as him.

from this money i was able to move us into our first apartment, literally a hole in the wall. it was near Beb Fetouah, not far from the apartment i keep for You now. i had already started to build a reputation in that neighborhood, after my second trip to Katema, when i could afford to take away even more goods. it was neighborhoods away from Uncle, whose profits were starting to decline as his clients became my own. i was young and city people couldn't read the hunger in my eyes. they trusted me. we stole away from him and i imagine it was like a rug taken from under his feet.

eventually i got our current place, a room with electricity running through the walls and a view of the whole medina from the roof. it was some three years since we had left the village and i was living a life my parents could never even have imagined—the convenience of water at my fingertips, a room that illuminated at the tap of a button. in Fes there was a man who came in the early hours of the morning to sweep the streets clean, so that i could leave shining plastic wrappers right where i had finished with them and find them whisked away when i awoke. the streets themselves were lit, a melon-colored glow that carried me home at night. there was even a night watchman on our street who twirled a big menacing stick before him, keeping the good people of Beb Fetouah safe from rascals like me. it was far from the darkness i had known at night as a boy in the country, darkness that bit at my toes and tried to steal them. darkness that swallowed the sound of your voice when you cried out. at night in the village where i grew up, i used to run my hands along my body to make sure i was still there, and that the darkness hadn't eaten me. city people don't know this darkness. not being able to see a few feet in front of you—grateful for a pale cloud or two at night to amplify the light of the moon. if our new environment frightened You You didn't show it. i can only call it courage that i saw in You as You adjusted to life in the city. its pace became your pace. sometimes you'd lead me to a stall somewhere where the juiciest persimmons could be found that had been unknown to me. i can't deny your ability to adapt. that's special about You, how your form will shift to fit where You find yourself. everyone doesn't have that, some are unable to ever escape their fixed natures to learn how to be somewhere new, or to learn who to be when life offers them surprises. months after we got our place, i bought another apartment in Lidoo, in the new town, where i kept a beautiful Senegalese girl who had crossed the dessert all the way into Morocco on her two bare feet, two feet that i kissed on nights when i could spare to be away from You. i kept another apartment for the daughter of a farmer in Katema, who i brought to Fes from her family's home, and she would comb my hair with her fingers and a little bit of cooking oil. yet despite these things, these things that i needed—so what if i'm not above desire, so what if my flesh still needs flesh—You were always first in my heart, and my love for You was the love of a brother for his sister. i kept You pure and safe from the corruption of the world, kept the door locked so You were always safe. i tried to even keep you safe from my own corruption (don't think i didn't already suspect that the city was creeping into me, changing my form). but under my protection, your cheeks grew fat and acquired a healthy shine.

love You had in your heart, tenderness that could undeniably draw people do you, you spilled over into your care for the herbs we grew. i could see as You watered and tended to them that it was out of a deep wellspring of compassion, a desire to share yourself and to see something outside yourself thriving. You'd come in from a walk now and then and in your eyes i could see the flicker of the dreams that had passed through your mind inspired by what You'd seen along your way. someone you'd seen had touched your heart in that special part of it only i knew, the part that deeply saw the needs of others and longed to connect to them, and did find its ways of connecting with them and leaving them changed. and although You still didn't speak a word, your posture was human. your mind was human. You were thriving.

and that's because of me. would You have wanted to waste away in that village in the desert, damned as the devil my family thought You were? or would You have preferred that i'd never even rescued You from the wilderness, and given You a human nature to match your form?

4

My cousin asked for a second turntable. she likes to play her music for You, but i couldn't imagine what she needed another record player for—to play twice as loud? God help us.

even though i go to see You almost every day, i don't feel any closer to You than i did the day i first we met. it draws my attention to my own failings. i've been a person of words, and You're wordless—how could i ever have hoped to connect with You? i don't even have the means. on Talaa Kabira, at an electronics shop lorded over by a white-haired man with thick glasses and a fraying tweed blazer, i found a used record player. it was nestled among some Lebanese records whose jackets had faded and yellowed, organized with total anarchy. when that man dies, i'm sure his business will die with him; how will he ever transmit that system of organization to a successor?

my parents slip money into my pockets sometimes, as they have since i was a boy. one night Aisha and i came to find You sitting in the darkness. your eyes were wide awake and seemed almost luminescent in the black room, seemed even to project light. it gave me an eerie feeling. i tried the light switch but realized that the power had been cut out. so it was me who, after asking the people who lived in your building about the electric company, paid the bill so that You could have the lights back.

i'm trying to be some kind of a provider to You, to handle your food and basic needs. otherwise, all i can do is watch and listen—a new kind of listening, for me, because You never speak.

i do listen to that music too now. not because i like it, but because i'm there. and because i can see that it means something to You, and i like to watch the expression of fascination that comes over your face as You're discovering something new in it.

on a rainy day, i present the second record player to my cousin and she gives me a tight, sloppy hug. i wrestle her arms away from me. she sets the record player on the floor next to the other one and motions You next to her. the two of you are there for two hours—and i find myself transfixed too, unable to move from my place on the sofa.

Aisha's music is car exhaust and desire circling upward into the sky to rest like haze somewhere between heaven and earth--God doesn't want it. i've never cared for it, but i sit as You convert it into something else entirely by your operation of the two record players. she must have shown you how to use them but the ownership of the motion is yours. You hunch over the turntables in deep concentration that sometimes makes your tongue stick out of your mouth while you're unaware of it for how lost in focus you've become. your touch of the needle moving it from record to record delicate and swift, loving like someone would use with a baby bird or a precious living creature. suddenly it's music that sings of Fes, that smells like our streets. suddenly it's music that sounds the way i remembered crying as a little boy, alone in my bed at night and overwhelmed by darkness. suddenly the voices of these men, who speak a strange language, are woven on top of one another so that they seem to be speaking with my voice, in a language so secret i've never had the courage to give it words. i want to cry, to tunnel back through darkness to a time when i wasn't afraid to cry. and unwillingly, i'm taken back to the dark room where i was questioned, the night i was taken to prison for making a joke—for forgetting that Fes is a mirror where any mistake you make can be magnified back to you. i'm taken back to the metallic taste of blood in my mouth—the slap of a man's hand on my face, a man wearing a silver ring that chipped my tooth as it came down on my mouth. i didn't have words then to explain myself. i searched for the words that would convince them of my innocence, but all i could find in myself was shame. i soiled myself and a stain was drawn through to my pants, wet-hot and acrid.

I start to feel an anger drawn from me, listening to You spin music.

they sent me to Fes at the beginning of this December and told me i could come back when the second half of the school year started. i wasn't going to school and they couldn't make me—i couldn't make myself. they didn't know what to do with me, and it was because i had become something strange to them. i had shown my unfitness for that country's bounty by catching the most contagious of American diseases, despair.

i had this one vision of coming up to Bone's house with a 9 millimeter, just like in that song. it just seemed like justice. i drew the gun on a piece of notebook paper so i could look at it. they found it and got scared, thought i was crazy.

i had began to dream of guns, to imagine myself firing one, and i told my mother i was saving money to kill that boy. i really meant it. i didn't really mean it. i really meant it. the day i erased his name from my body for the last time, i'd seen him in another isle of a bodega by my house, laughing, his arm around this Chinese girl. from then i started plotting his death in a thousand ways every day, until i could find hardly anything else to fill my head. i had stopped going to classes to sit on benches next to crazy ladies talking to themselves, or even just to lie in bed watching shadows pass over me all day until it was night. i'd abandoned Wanda and most of my friends—because most of my friends weren't my friends, just people i'd stood with in dark rooms, each of us hoping the night around us concealed our loneliness. it was unlikely that i'd pass to the next grade at the end of the year. my father came home for lunch one day and found me sitting at the kitchen table. he looked at me and said: 'so you don't go to school now.' i couldn't answer him, so i stared into my cup, and he didn't say anything else but he looked lost. he looked like he'd gone to sleep as a young man and woke up old, like Rip Van Winkle, woken up old and in a strange land, in a body he didn't recognize, and here was some girl claiming to be his own flesh. how could i not have failed them?

now that i'm here i understand how alien i am to them. i understand that nothing in their Fessi childhoods prepared them for the kind of kid i would be. when my mother was a girl, did she think she'd grow up to be a lady like Khalti Miriam?—fat and beautiful, with thick silver bangles down her arm, her eyes teary from the powdered khol she used to line them, French perfume and a manicure her only aesthetic concessions to the ex-conqueror…with a husband she never touches and a house she never leaves? did she think she would have a daughter like Khalti's friends have, meek-smiled and shy-eyed, wiping crumbs of bread from the table after every meal? instead she got me, a girl who spent long nights in exile from her on the sofas of strangers, far across the deadly spiked towers of a sparkling, raging, lonesome city. as instead of growing into a happy matron, she found herself exiled, too, thin with worry, fifteen years far from the land where she was born.

i was never a good student like Rachid, but i understand him too, and i understand why he can't go to school. his parents are good with him and they let him do what he needs to do. i wish my parents respected me like that.

i didn't object to coming to Fes. i felt numb and unwanted, and tired. the only boy who'd ever looked at me didn't want me and neither did my parents. at the airport in New York snow was sloping sideways out the sky, and i shuffled one foot in front of the other, methodically turning the blanket of powder on the ramp to slush as i approached the plane. i wanted to shed my own life like snakeskin, and i didn't really care what kind of new skin was peeking under there, raw and pink. i sat next to an old lady in hijab and Chanel glasses on the plane, and she let me have her pack of butter to put on the hard little roll of bread they'd given us. i cut with that plane into the enormous cloud of dust that cloaks my parents' country. an old train groaned under me, from Casa to Fes, and i let myself be carried past desolate shantytowns and hills with waving grasses, and past the young boys who stood in salute to progress, looking into our windows as we passed in dull t-shirts with faded American logos and broad bare feet, their hair whipped on end by the rush of the passing train. first thing that struck me about my parents' country from that train was all the men sitting around in dusty cafes with nothing to do, their faces creased from all that sitting, that whole life of waiting. at Sidi Kacem some kids hopped onto the train and gripped at it sides, their mouths wide open in gaping, reckless smiles. they beat on the sides of the train and twisted their faces and pressed close when another train passed and we all gasped for them to see them riding in the narrow sliding corridor. they rode a half an hour with us before they got off at some other small town.

Rachid's father met me at the train station in Fes with their servant Abdelkarim. they were standing in the lobby under a framed photograph of the king shaking the hand of a soccer player in uniform; the king himself looking like a rockstar, or a saint, in aviator-frame sunglasses, an immaculate white suit, and shiny white patent leather shoes. beneath him, the two old men who had showed up to greet me seemed stooped and pitifully mortal, and one of them raised his hand and called my name, tentative in his speculation that this weirdo was his niece. i handed over my one suitcase full of clothes and hugged my other suitcase, full of records, to my body.

a ragged beggar hustling outside the station hailed

us a taxi, ran it down like his life depended it, a tattered matador circling a fuming metal bull. as we got into the cab my uncle asked the beggar how much he wanted for his trouble. 'whatever God has written,' the man said, and accepted a two-dirham piece before our door clicked closed and we passed through the sad and sleepy modern part of the city, every door shut, every light out, every street empty. only a mint seller's donkey-drawn cart beside us at a stoplight, with a boy in the back gathering what was left at the end of the day, mint leaves blown by the wind to the asphalt before us, the smell of mint blown through my half-open window with the oncoming night.

we got out of the cab and the giant doorway of blue Beb Boujloud stood before us, and we entered the old city, the medina. here, people were still out, and lights were bright on my face. wild music came from some of the stalls, horns and bells and high-pitched cries. i shrank away from a camel's severed head hanging from the butcher's stall; the thing looked still alive, its long eyelashes closed as if in sleep, a bundle of herbs shoved decoratively between its teeth. shouldered by the crowd of people, we passed stacked cages of chickens with dirty feathers. i'm used to the commotion of a city but nothing had prepared me for the medina at night. why hadn't my parents told me about Fes' noise before, or about the assault of its smells on your senses? somehow these were points their nostalgia had missed. where was the majestic city, the ancient center of learning and art? was this it? a tired old man passed on a sick grey horse, the beast's great tongue lolling limp from its frothing mouth.

that next morning, the first morning i'd woken up in Fes, Khalti had come to inspect me bearing tea and sweet pastries. she'd smiled at me, a well-bred smile not unlike that of her sister, my mother. she had felt my feet beneath the blanket, gripped them firmly. it was an affectionate gesture, but also one of possession. she was examining the shape of this new thing that had come to her with her sister's face. she'd said to me then, her eyes becoming very small and black, 'the last time i saw your mother i was squeezed against her hugely pregnant belly in the back of a very small car.'

i looked at her. even at this hour, her hair was nicely done. there were the beginnings of words in the back of my throat, but, like You, i knew it wasn't my place to speak. so Khalti continued: 'we were going with thousands of others, many on foot, to reclaim the Sahara for the king. it was for poor people, this march, but your mother persuaded me that we should go. one last adventure together before she took the grandest adventure of them all.' her voice was controlled, quietly dignified. i wiped the crust of sleep from an eye with my thumb. with a small voice, unsure of my Arabic, i asked her, 'to join my father in New York?'

'of course.'

'she didn't know him very well,' i said. it was also a question, and a judgment.

'child,' Khalti answered me, 'there are many things you don't know very well, but that doesn't make them less real.'

she said it and in the remnant of a dream i'd had—a recurring one, a fantasy—fire blazed around me as i gripped a gun, look into the eyes of someone—someone who has had Bone's face but whose features have washed out into anonymity—and shoot him dead through the heart, and as he falls there's an arc of blood in his wake. but i come back to the cold room as it fills with your warm resonance.

i haven't touched the record player since i put it down next to You. as if You can read the music written in the grooves of records by touch, You choose the right sounds without me and blend them together between the two turntables, like someone i've passed in the medina weaving a carpet on a loom, crossing colors until they sing. outside rain falls. You look at me, growing sure of yourself.

By the time lightning from the evening's storm floods my cell with light, illuminating the bareness of the walls, i have regained the conviction that i'm alone, that when i speak there's no one there. i cannot recognize myself when i look down at my own body.

in the next moment i can consider it possible that You are as much a prisoner as i am. that we have kept You prisoner since the day we insisted that You become one of us. that i continued to imprison You in the apartment near Beb Fetueh. that the city itself is a prison for You. that even these words keep You captive. if anyone else can free You in ways that i can't, let them.

in shame, i surrender to sleep as the outside storm's cold wind seeps into the cell to chill my bones.

II.
BREAD

...

"No one guided me to myself. I am the guide.
Between desert and sea, I am my own guide to myself.

...I am what I have spoken to the words:
Be the place where
my body joins the eternity of the desert,
Be, so that I may become my words."

—Mahmoud Darwish, from "A Rhyme for the Odes."

1

The door is never closed, so anyone can wander in. people do: first the little boy that lives downstairs, crumbs of bread on his cheeks and jam at the corner of his mouth. his name is Yusef, and he's come after the curious sound that wafts like scent from your apartment. You look up at him and smile, and he kneels beside us. two days after the rainstorm, the air holds a new cool, a chill that stands the hairs on the back of my neck. Rachid has already left so it's just us, me and You—and Yusef, who sits on the floor with us, in fascination of the spinning record. he reaches a fat finger to touch it, to line the grooves with the ridges of his little fingerprints, but You pull his hand away.

without Rachid here, You ease up your body, leave your poor cuticles unbitten for a few hours. You begin to own this space again. it's your space: Sheep's house, not Rachid's, not even Aisha's. before we invaded—Rachid and me—the small apartment was yours and You must have filled it with yourself, before we crowded You to the edges and You became a watched thing, a looked-at thing, scared under the glares of our observation. though i sometimes have the suspicion that someone taught You to be scared. poor girl without a name—who was it who said You were unworthy of a name? and without a voice, You can't name yourself. maybe your name has silent syllables.

first Yusef, then Fatema, his mother, coming upstairs after him. she's young, can't be much older than me. i recognize her as someone i passed on Talaa once, wearing jellaba and a scarf over head, someone i had apologized to for nearly knocking over in my hurry back to Khalti's house from a vegetable market. she's apprehensive about entering at first, resting her toe in its sandal at the invisible line of the doorstep, but Yusef says 'come in mama' and your face agrees and i laugh and say 'welcome'. she sits on the banquette, clearly tired, looking child-like with her head uncovered, her face fragile under grave eyebrows.

through the small window—no glass, no curtain, only thin iron bars—a cloud of swallows covers the sky, then the muezzin hollers sunset from the mosque on the block and on its ancient cue the sun dips past sight. Fatema takes little Yusef's hands and the two dance a jerky waltz, Yusef riding the tops of her feet.

there's a need to cultivate a sense of my own mystery, that grows in me in Fes—a city where you're not even safe from spying eyes on your own rooftop, where you are always a watcher, always watched, watching yourself watching and watching yourself watched. trying to shield yourself from your neighbor's cry of shame by flicking the mirror of shame back at them, your deadly weapon. (i am never seen with boys and only once did i try to breech the bastion of the café terrace—one time at Batha, coming from your house, at a café where i saw this French lady sitting; i sat too, but when i ordered my coffee the waiter looked at me funny, and i forgot that the rules are different for brown ladies.

(but i'm out late these days and i don't behave, never behaved. just give me the city, any city, any place where families pack themselves into spaces too small, any place where there's someone on a corner with a shifty eye, any place with a big bad night to get lost in. i have to admit to myself lately, as this city grows into me like moss in the cracks of a forgotten building ((filling me without meaning to, me filled without having known i was empty)), that a part of me only feels at home in a city when i'm hiding somewhere in it, away from home—and though your apartment is only a twenty minute walk from Khalti's house, your cramped room sometimes feels the farthest i could possibly be from that old broken down house, laden with wool carpets, perfumed with incense so as to try and convince itself, when it looks into the mirror of the city, that it's not so old and not so broken down. and You, nameless, voiceless, are the farthest i've ever been from any one in my family. farther than the Chinese who own the restaurant that sends the smell of greasy chicken up and down the block. further than the long knotted names of the Eastern European kids in my class. You are far enough that perhaps You're something other than human. is this why You have no name but the word for an animal? when i'm with You, we speak the language that i remember speaking to the puppy my parents got for me when i was little, hit by a car just a few weeks after i got it. You are something back and back, before humanity.)

because this city is tangled and growing in on itself. behind any door is a fragrant garden with petals of jasmine in its shadowed pools; or an addict smoking himself into the night; or a thin mother with countless children tugging at her feet; or a circle of musicians drumming themselves into a trance, drawing the corruption from their bodies by surrendering to the voices of old gods. pick a door and see what you get—except that they are all closed to you, not locked with bolts but with unspoken rules. so it is that the same women who barely have enough uncovered skin between their hairlines and chins to flick a stare of shame at my choice of dress, ever inadequate by standards of modesty here, bare their own bodies without shame in the communal baths. because this city cultivates its own mystery and only laughs at you when you search for the truth behind the riddle—or locks you away, tortured, behind the door that hides the prison.

'you're not Moroccan?,' Fatema asks me, a question that i know drips in silent tremors from the lips of almost everyone in my daily orbit. she considers herself lucky to be so close and so brave as to pose it.

'my parents are Moroccan,' i tell her.

'which is better, your country or our country?' i can never tell if people here are suspicious of my foreignness of in awe of it.

'there isn't one better,' i tell Fatema, my diplomatic, canned answer.

'what is this music?,' she asks, lifting Yusef and bouncing him in time on her hip.

'it's called hip-hop,' i tell her, and in consideration of the term she turns the corners of her mouth down.

'it's strange but i like it,' Fatema says, almost bashfully, almost as if it makes her think of herself as a traitor. 'is she making it?,' she asks, pointing to Sheep—who before had maybe been her stunted, reclusive neighbor: a pair of eyes from the window above hers. 'yes,' i tell her. *yes, You tell her*. i almost hear it.

Fatema brushes crumbs from the mouth of her son and taps her foot rhythmically. 'do you like our music too?,' she asks me. she has already made the separation for me, between my Eastern parts and my Western ones; she has chosen my side, and she has positioned herself at the other shore.

'my family listens to it and it's nice,' i say, thinking of the wailing women from the middle east that my uncle puts on in the evenings, their voices swelling with the kinds of plaintive emotions people where i'm from don't even have anymore. and i think of the wedding Khalti and uncle's neighbors had a few nights ago, and the complicated violin melodies that rose over the wall from the classical Fessi orchestra that was hired. and i think of the elephant-nosed horns and wide tambourines of the Essaoua troupe i'd passed that morning.

and i can't help but to begin to think, too, of the kind of music i hear coming from shops sometimes, or floating from cafes where young men gather (i, uninvited, never join them). soaring voices, lush keyboards—and this is dangerous music, i can tell, music that carries desire too freely.

'does she play *rai* music?,' Fatema asks me.

'*opinion* music?' i say.

Fatema laughs, not mockingly but cheerfully, 'wait,' she says, and sets the boy down and leaves for a minute to go downstairs. she returns quickly hands me a record. 'it comes from Algeria,' she tells me.

You remove the record from its sleeve, on which is printed a photograph of someone named Cheb with a moustache and Jeri curl. You smooth your palm over the surface of the record, reading the coding of the music like Braile. for a moment You stop the music, then You replace one record with Fatema's, and blend it seamlessly with Afrikka Bambataa on the other turntable.

Fatema's face lights. she claps her hands as the music plays. 'Bravo alik!,' she tells You. Yusef claps his hands too, in imitation of his mother.

'Cheb Housni,' Fatema tells me, as her eyelids flutter, moved by the music. 'even children know the words to his songs. he sings with courage. he makes three cassette tapes a day.'

'three a day? such a person,' i offer, 'must know exactly what he's doing in this world. he must know that he won't be here forever.'

Fatema weighs this with a sideways smile, and then she leaves for a moment to bring us bowls of harira. we all sit and eat together, and then she leaves for the evening to put Yusef to bed. i figure i should leave too. it's become late. i come home as they are whispering their prayers into the early morning from the mosque, turn my key in the door and wiggle it just so. it creaks. i pull off my sneakers and slide into my houseshoes. so i sneak into and out of houses now. this city must be my home.

i cross the central courtyard. there is half a jagged moon in the sky and it polishes the stone floor, shines it so that i see my own vague reflection in it. i look down as i walk, at my feet in their yellow shoes, then up again at the thin light from the sky.

down again at my feet, and beside them are Khalti's, the carefully painted feet in their slippers.

'what are you doing?,' she asks me.

i look up, directly into her face. 'i'm going to bed.'

'it's almost time to wake up, and you're just entering the house?'

i give her an epic sigh, the kind i haven't had the opportunity to practice in at least two weeks now. 'Rachid does whatever he wants.'

'don't talk to me about my son. your mother should be ashamed of herself. fifteen years without touching the soil of her homeland, and this is the replacement for herself she sends?'

it wounds me, as though the force of her words has struck my body. i am no one's replacement. but i quickly gather my breath against the shock, enough to blow out my lips dramatically, raising a puff of hair from my face. i know it makes her angrier, but it feels good, as though i'm returning to myself, filling a familiar role again.

'Aisha,' my aunt says to me, almost pleadingly, 'don't you want to be a good girl?'

but we are not good girls, are we? You and me. no one has ever told me i was a good girl. i see myself as a fuzzy haired little kid, on a swing at the playground, kicking my legs into the air, showing my teeth to the sun. i see You, binding the strangers in a room to one another with one baseline, the music not yours, but now yours, You quietly and newly comfortable with being not-so-, or more-than-, human.

'so what i've heard is true,' Saiid, a former classmate, says to me, 'you came back.'

acid rises from my chest, and a brief fear. this classmate

of mine never struck me as someone i can trust. he's bitter and conniving, and his father's in the police. was he the one who betrayed me? just to have my space in class? the dawn of this possibility fixes me to my spot on the post office's stairs.

'of course i did,' i tell him, 'i'm not a criminal.' and if anyone wants to charge me with thinking dangerous things, or having concerns for a world that isn't mine, or wanting voiceless hungry mouths (only You! only You.) to be fed—that person is a liar.

'but,' Said asks me, 'you won't be coming back to school?'

i shake my head. 'it's not for me anymore. i've seen other things.'

'like what? the inside of a prison cell?' he's smug. i can't seem to understand why. it strikes me that his smugness masks unease.

'not as beautiful as the inside of a library, i suppose, but we have to take what God gives us.'

'and people think you're some kind of martyr now, don't they?'

'i just want peace, silence.'

'you don't want revenge on the person who did that to you?'

'just peace.'

Saiid looks dissatisfied with my answer—and this in itself is satisfying to me. despite the fact that i'm not paying him any attention, he yaps at my back, 'next year i'll probably graduate first in our class, without you there.'

i have come to the post to mail a package. from a shop across the street, Saiid saw me and waved. i didn't wave back. i hoped he would disappear. instead he approached me, and stood in line with me until the counter. the postal worker refused to let me mail my package, because the return address did not exactly match the name on my carte national. aggravated, i sat on the steps of the post office. Saiid sat with me and listened to me complain—in a whisper, because i won't be fool enough to be overheard again. and i didn't even know if it was he who had betrayed me in the first place. the saddest truth is that no one at all can be trusted. to be in his presence now viscerally sickens me.

Saiid looks down at his nails. 'well, somebody has to have something.'

'what's that supposed to mean?'

'we can't all just have nothing. some one has to have. if not you, then me.'

'what?,' i turn to really look at Saiid for the first time, into his small eyes, the purple slash of his mouth. i squint, trying to read his intentions between the bars of my frustration at the post office.

but Saiid hops to his feet. without attempting any kind of pleasant goodbye, he's turned a corner and gone. after a minute of sitting there i loose my train of thought and watch two dirty, scrappy cats have a tug-of-war over a piece of meat on the ground, fallen out of someone's sandwich. then i rise to my own feet, clutching the unsent package.

i will go to You today. the general strike is tomorrow and i want to be safely indoors, away from it. i'll take the long route to You, because walking's nice on days like today, when it's winter and the streets are bare, between two and five in the afternoon.

i remember being a small boy and walking down some street, a long, cool corridor—maybe it was around this time of year. and with my memory's eye i look up at a tiny window and see a face, that shyly turns away when it notices me.

or else it was the heat of summer—i'll change the lighting and the weather in my memory—that hour when the streets are dead and everyone sleeps. i pass two women talking as they walk, enveloped in the fabric of their *haiks* from head to foot, with only their eyes showing, and the murmur of the long veils that move around them adds its voice to their conversation. and i pass a woman i've never seen before, sitting in her doorway with her unbaked bread dough on a tray—*my son, take this dough to the bakers, and may God reward you with goodness*, and i balance it on an arm and run as fast as i can while keeping it balanced. i never get to taste the hot bread, that breaks softly, but i imagine it, my mouth waters for it.

no one talks about Fes' quiet, the peace you can know down some dark secret street, coiled so deeply in the center of the medina that you almost go backwards in time to get there. Fes, if you let it, gives you peace like you haven't known since you floated in the womb, peace like you won't know until the silence of your grave.

Sheep You're a quiet place in Fes, a dark place i can run to. your total silence—even your eyes are silent sometimes. in the center of everything, You are quiet. the strange music you play is not, but You exude a peace and calm from within it and in its way it only seems to draw calm further from You.

i shake my head as i make my way to You, greeting no one, letting the noise of the streets (man beating a donkey with a stick, calling *watch out watchout)* wash over me. i can't drag myself out into those streets tomorrow. i won't be one of those who robs Fes of its peace.

The cell begins to fill, ten at a time. this morning i had the urge to pray and searched for the words i'd been taught as a boy, the words that reach heaven. but then i remembered how far i am from God and laughed at my own attempt.

within two hours it is impossible to move: bodies upon bodies, bodies undulating with muscle, and voices pushed at once from the bodies in such confusion that i can't make out what they're saying. i find myself standing, wedged between a man with an accent from the north and a boy who only came up to my chest. i put a hand on the boy's head and asked him what was going on. i leaned close to his mouth and he blew words into my ear, so clear that they cut through all the shouting and panic around us: 'the king's army is out in the streets,' he says to me. overhearing us, the northerner said, 'i just stepped outside, i just stepped outside and they took me. it's hell. God help us, God save us.'

i can perceive a deep hunger moaning in the bellies of each person standing with me, fifty or so hungers that begin to merge into one hunger. a guard shouts my name and calls me to him, from the front of the room. i wave my hand above the crowd and shoulder through. one man lifts his arm so that i can pass under. one man tries to punch me in the gut as i pass him, but my reflex is quick—i catch his fist in one hand and shove it back at him.

i'm at the front of the room. 'Aziz Aziz?,' he asks me. he asks me the date that i entered and i tell him. i remember it well. 'you're the right one,' he says:

'you're free.'

'say it again, sir?'

'you didn't hear me? get out of here. now we have a real threat to worry about.'

strange as it is to confess, i'm a little offended not to be considered a real threat. but i will take my freedom, and bring it home to You.

it is a different city that i am returned back into. smashed and burning. just outside, as i advance maybe 30 meters from the prison door, i see two men lugging a color television, hoisting it between themselves and moving as quickly as they can, waddling like some four-legged cyborg. one third machine and two thirds man. behind them the shattered window of an electronics shop, now framed by jagged glass teeth. inside i see others scavenging the rubble, picking out expensive things for themselves. some run away quickly—one boy falls face-first, the bones of his nose crushing beneath him, but gets up and jets off, a radio held high above his head and blood dripping to his chin victoriously.

the scream of a little girl. a woman's ululation—joy or fear? and i seem to move through a smoke or a fog that cloaks Fes—a piece of heaven descended to earth, or is the city on fire? destroy it, then. from my own belly comes a cry that rips me open. what better welcome back into the free world than this rage? i feel in a second that it will overcome me, and that i will surrender to it, and that in doing so i become part of a mad dance with all of Fes, the ancient walls crushed beneath our frenzied feet. i don't know what i'm doing, and the joy of that is sweeter than anything—sweeter than anything except the moment i see your face again. i am coming to You, but i will let this chaos take me there.

i cross a street and stand looking behind me, at the crowd on the corner where i'd been, all anxious hands and eager feet. across from them, a line of soldiers. in unison they release tear gas into the crowd, all its members set falling to their knees, crouching, grown men reduced to tears. not me, though.

beneath my skin i write a list of demands in imaginary electric ink: i will be swept into this, into the fuming city and the ungodly new crimes that wait for me there, and for my trouble i want a number of impossible things: a return to my boyhood's innocence, the wearying years of my life in this city censored in my memory by God's careful hands; the feeling of humanity that was robbed from me as i rotted in that cell; the feeling of dignity i had before i knew i was poor; the feeling of purity i had before i touched money; but money, still, uncountable coins and paper notes; the feeling of pride i had before i knew i wasn't an Arab; and You, beside me and filling me with myself. and in wanting all these things i know myself to be a criminal, i know myself to be contradictory, i know myself to be undeserving. as a boy, new to Fes, i remember feeling that city people were complicated: their changes of dress, their elaborate routine, the endless drama they find among the hundreds of faces they pass every day (in my village there were no strangers, anonymity was impossible—where in Fes anonymity is merely difficult, not because the city is small, but because it's infinite the way a mirror becomes infinite when another mirror faces it) their horses dressed in clothes just like them, and ringing bells at their feet in each step. their automobiles, live silver dragons on electronic reins—

there goes an automobile now, to my left, up in flames, a black skeleton against plumes of fire, the men who did it scattering like pigeons down the street.
and look at me, one of the city folk, one of the criminals: one of the complicated.

my legs have barely enough time to get used to the new ground beneath my feet. this new city is like nothing i've ever imagined. i thought the world had ended when i was cornered and shut into prison, but it seems the world will keep on ending.

When i woke up i knew the city had changed because i was now a part of it. it had become like a part of me extended in a thousand directions, my own emotions broadcast on millions of faces.

since i shattered Khalti's image of me, coming in late, there is no breakfast waiting for me in the morning, only yesterday's stale loaf. i sit down in my socks in the salon. maybe i'll go out and have breakfast by myself.

i leave, quietly shutting the door behind me. asking for no permission. for the first time, i think I'll actually sit down and order at a café. why shouldn't i? i have a right to this city. i have the right to live as i want in it. (this despite—to spite—the distinct feeling i've always had that there are not rights here, only what you dare to get away with).

it's mid-morning, not early. the last fringes of the night's cold dangle in the air and in half an hour they'll have been replaced with that delicate heat that comes lightly into Fes in winter, a precarious heat easily robbed by the whims of a breeze or a thick enough cloud over the sun. this time of morning the medina's streets should be live, cats already crouched beneath the carcasses on the butcher's hook, the odd tardy kid hobbling under his backpack in his rush to school. but oddly,

every street is deserted. the cops who can usually be found slouching in their blue uniforms on every corner, keeping their ears open for treason and their hands open for bribes, have all been replaced by soldiers. menacing guns and militant posture. no one is in any shop. even the dirty little cats are hiding. even the rats. i leave the gates of the medina and cross into the new town. an army tank looms at a roundabout, massive and foreboding, and i pass under its shadow.

the new town is quiet too. it's a suspicious quiet, like

the transparent skin over warm milk; ready to be broken.

i find myself at the avenue named for the king, still in search of an open café, and down the avenue i stand to watch a procession of hundreds of people, the first real life i've seen in the city all morning. they carry signs on banners i can't quite make out. the sidewalk to either side of their route is lined with their main audience, a solemn row of olive-uniformed soldiers. i can't read in Arabic, so i can't make any meaning of the broad, swift strokes of paint on the banners. i tug at the jacket of a man on the street. 'cherif,' i ask him, 'what's all this about?'

'bread. hunger, cherifa,' he tells me, looking very teacherly in his wool turtleneck sweater and sports jacket. he's taken a lot of care in choosing his clothes to watch the protest today: clean black shoes, prudently parted hair. 'the strike against the price of food and the state of unemployment in the country has been planned for months. where have you been?' he manages to make me feel embarrassed for not having known in advance while still looking on me with a protective concern, the corners of his eyes crinkling kindly.

in a few minutes i'll watch this stranger, all dressed up to meet his death, fall to the ground in a pool of blood.

one of the crowd's slogans catches momentum. people who live in apartments above the streets hang out of their open windows, catch the chant and chant with them, until it roars into the sky and even i'm chanting, words i don't know.

now there's an anger in the words. now the crowd stops, hundreds of pairs of eyes looking hundreds of soldiers in the face. a man from the countryside with a wool jellaba and yellow turban and sun-creased face faces a young soldier, rears his head back, and spits on him. the soldier takes his gun and shoots him point-blank, the sound echoing a thousand times and chaos breaks out—

there are screams, there are many people down. it's not something i've never imagined. but it's something—

the disorder, the fear rippling the air in shockwaves—i never really believed i'd be a part of...a taut string inside me snaps in two with a resounding vibration, one pitch that begins to occupy a space between my ears.

it has nothing to do with me. this is not my country. here i am, though.

even though i eat well everyday, don't i know hunger? haven't i lost? i think of how everyone who loves me reneges on me.

and i think of your silence. maybe there are things that You wish You could say. these things, then, faintly imagined, given language in the quickening of my heart, in the route of blood through my body—become my cry into battle. i will reach You.

so i let the crowd carry me and it's only an hour or later when i stop briefly to realize how little fear there is in me. every car on every street is exploding. because in Fes cars only belong to people you don't know, mythical people, the ones who exist somewhere beyond your sight, sitting around having more than you do.

i see property smashed—because property, too, belongs to those invisible ones, the haves to your have-not. every window it seems. and i see people younger than me die. soon i've seen so many people die in such a short time that i can feel a caul grow around my heart, and i can identify it as a thing that will never leave, never again allow me a real sensitivity to the world around me. two kids who blow up a car shot in the back with precision. a woman dropped from her balcony to the ground after her body's made limp by the bullet.

the city has entered into a timelessness, has evolved into consequence-less-ness. people running around like it's the last day on earth and they'll never be judged, and they can escape any crime unconcerned—the man over there hugging a reluctant woman tight to him, clutching at the fat on her body.

there's open fire again and i duck under the table of a deserted restaurant, bullets fly within feet of me (unreal!). i didn't see that someone had set his sights on the table as a refuge before me. hugging his knees beside me in the shadowy, cramped space is a man, vaguely young but with such severity in his eyes—in my parents' country either the city or the country can do it, make a man ageless like that. he's clean-shaved, but smells like he hasn't bathed in months.

ourbodiesnearlytouch. iapologizetohimfornothaving seen him, but he waves his hand. 'the world's tranquil,' he tells me, a colloquialism people sometimes use to accept apologies. usually it doesn't ring under circumstances quite so ironic.

weareonlyafewblocksawayfromyourapartmentnow. we hear the protracted moans of someone dying in agony and try not to imagine the visual details of it. he asks me my name.

'Aisha,' i tell him, 'and you?'

'Aziz,' he says.

the severity of the situation forces an immediate intimacy on us. i've just learned his name and already feel that i've known him for years. 'will we die?,' i ask him in a whisper. he answers the only way anyone here ever answers a question like that: 'that's for God to decide.'

we are silent for a second as we listen to something explode. then Aziz continues his thought, 'but if you stay with me i'll protect you.'

'if i stay with you we'll both die together, but that's about it. i don't need protection.'

there's something dangerous about Aziz and i like dangerous people. maybe it's only the danger of the circumstances that makes him seem that way. maybe if i close one eye, then open it and close the other, i'll be able to somehow distinguish between Aziz's danger and Fes' danger—but maybe they will always seem hard to separate from one another. at any rate something about him makes me doubt his ability to protect me. either this, or wanting to refuse protection is just the same stubbornness that never fails to get me into trouble—close the left eye, open, close the right, open. no difference.

it's gotten quiet outside—that deadly silence again. i relax some muscles. 'let's go,' Aziz says to me, and so we go. better to have a buddy anyway. no one wants to die alone.

we cross the train tracks into the chaabi neighborhoods on the rim of the city. neighborhoods slapped over barren soil and trash heaps, Aziz tells me, because the medina couldn't contain all its poor. Aziz finds metal rods on the ground at an abandoned construction site we pass and he grabs one. the next window, he smashes. a shop full of used things. ahead of him, i crawl into the broken window. i find a nice pair of gold earrings and put them through my ears. i toss Aziz a gold watch and crawl out.

in the distance, on a hill, the hotel Les Merinides burns. black smoke billows from it licked by tongues of flame. a boy runs past us. then another. Aziz stops him to ask where they're going.

'You can take anything you want from the hotel if you hurry before it's all gone!'

the boy runs past us, a loaf of bread in his hand. so the girl Aisha and i head up the hill to see what fortune can be ours.

there's something familiar in Aisha's face. it reminds me of someone i know but i can't place who. an old friend maybe. the resemblance, however vague, unsettles me, and for that reason i wouldn't for a second try to make an advance on her. don't misunderstand me. i am not lecherous.

Aisha's company is nice. i can tell she's not from around here and i sometimes struggle to understand her accent, though i'm not one to judge. Arabic isn't my first language either. walking with her through this chaos reminds me of You—makes me think of the days we spent together when i was just a kid in the country, when we'd try to ramble over the hills all the way to the horizon, turning back only after the sky was pitch black and reeling with stars. makes me remember our first day in Fes. You were my only friend. You still are. i'm coming to You, though i've gone far out of my way in this madness.

up the hill, through the ghettoes. if i'd planned Fes, i would have known better than to mash the rich and the poor together like that. too late for Fes, but not for me and Aisha—and thousands of others today.

we come up the burning mountain. we enter the skeletal building that once was a palatial hotel. the staff has fled and some of the wealthier guests have been killed by looters, the pearls ripped from around their necks, the rings jerked from their fingers. the flames glare reflected in the marble.

i want a television. just a small one, and it doesn't have to be color. we greet the people exiting through the revolving door loaded with new things: towels monogrammed with the hotel's red initials, furniture of rich dark wood, fine crystal glasses.

i tell Aisha she can stay downstairs.

and i tell her, 'you're a natural thief.'

'yeah?'

'you steal often?'

'no!,' she says quickly, taken aback by the idea, then, shly, 'do you?'

'i haven't in a long time.'

'this is kind of like a special occasion i guess.' she laughs. a car explodes in the parking lot of the hotel, framed in my view by the window behind her and it strikes me as festive, like fireworks.

upstairs in the hotel, in a looted room from whose broken window i can see the debris-ridden swimming pool, i stare into the vacant eyes of a dead Kuwaiti in his traditional dress—many foreign business people stay in this hotel, the kind of people who rightfully suspect that they might not return intact if they wandered too far from their luxurious enclosure, their protection from the reality of the country they came to on vacation, from whose grand windows the city is peaceful and still as a photograph. This man lies lifeless on his bed, as lifeless, it dawns on me, as i'll be one day. his neck is bruised, a sign that he's been strangled. shaking in the corner is a young boy. 'are you the murderer?' i ask him. he nods, but says in the Tashelhit Berber language, 'i'm not a murderer, i'm not a murderer.' he's from the region in the south where i grew up. in the tongue of my childhood i respond: 'then why did you do it?'

'they have so much,' he says.

'who?'

he can't answer. i go over to him and put a hand over his hand, to stop it from shaking. 'i thought he would have money, but i found nothing.'

we are all on intimate terms today, we strangers, and today i've found in me a compassion i rarely exercise; maybe it's just freedom, the relief of human contact again. the boy continues. 'there must be someone you can call to. you beg at God's window but he never looks down. you cry to the state but they beat you. you try the rich—'

'—but they're only human, just like you, and just like you, when they die, they're gone.'

'yes.'

'so you try to do something for yourself, and you find that you're powerless, just as knew you were from the beginning. what do we do, then?'

'do you know?'

i don't have anything honest to tell him. so i say, 'you just accept what you get. everything is written.'

he is calm now, breathing normally. 'and,' it occurs to me, 'you try to remember that just because someone has more than you doesn't mean he's a better man.'

he throws his arms around me, clinging to me like i'm his mother. 'what's your name?,' i ask him.

'Yedder.' when he says it, i feel a sharp pang, like someone's stuck a knife between my ribs: that was my name, when i was his age. Fes is a mirror, Sheep. it will rip your image from you and throw it back at you, shredded to nearly nothing.

Don't You look at me that way, i'm not a coward. it's to protect You that i'm staying indoors. it's to keep You safe.

we watch the city grow wild around us from the safety of the one-room apartment. it's Friday, the holy day. from the roof, i watch a man come out of the mosque below, wash his hands, then raise his fist to chant a slogan, and i watch him butted in the back of a head with a soldier's gun.

i'm not one of those foolish people. i won't have the cruel hand of the law come down on me again. as the sun sets, i can hear from the buzz in the alley below that it's become illegal for anyone to be out on the street. there's a curfew in place now, and anyone who breaks it—just by being outside—goes straight to jail.

even the mosque now, usually full of the faithful at sunset prayer on a Friday, is empty. but conversations come through the walls and i catch short questions:

how long will it last?

how many dead?

what have we done?

You begin to play your records. first a mournful mix, two songs blended together slowly. then the pace speeds up. the woman who lives downstairs walks through the door uninvited, and i start to say something to her about her intrusion—but i see that You recognize her, with a curious and inviting smile. she's a young woman and i know she has a gregarious little boy. she sways slowly to the music You play, dancing by herself. You turn the volume up.

the apartment fills, one by one, with strangers, dancing alone and with each other. old people in traditional clothes. women. children.

they stay all night. hardly a word is spoken, certainly not to me. i don't dance but i watch You, commander in the center of it all. exorcist of broken spirits.

You never look at me. never express any comfort with me. never express any welcome. i still want what You have, and You never see me, not when i'm in the same room as You, not when i'm next to You. i tried once to touch your hand but You drew away. not frightened, but actually repulsed. and yet i still—persistently, relentlessly, faithfully—*want what You have*. and i don't want to have to take it from You.

It's been more than twenty-four hours since i left Khalti's house in the medina. i barely noticed the new sun rising, i only looked around and it was day. somehow i have to make my way home. even if no one cares about me, at least someone might have noticed i'm gone. i want to find You today too, to know that you're ok.

the city is a war zone. an overturned tank here. another dead child there. everything flammable in flames. the disfigured body of a man beside me. all the movies i've seen have prepared me for scenes like this, filled me with vague fear of them. but none of them prepared me for the feeling of hollowness beyond all fear—an emotion beyond any emotion. to look at something that used to be a man and view it, coldly, as a hunk of flesh. to not have time to pity, to not have time to mourn. to move in instinctive self-preservation—not because you want to live but because you're still alive, against any conscious urge, rendered still forward by unconscious ones.

i still don't know who's fighting who or why. there's only one army, pitting its guns against the sticks and the knives and the sheer rage of thousands. the people fighting their government? the government fighting its people? any explanation of how things like this work has always been beyond me, like calculus.

i want to be distant from these kinds of things. i want them to stay locked in the memories of the old and in houses of entertainment. i want to know that they only happen in crazy, far away places—like this one?

here i am, not so far away from it. here i am in the place i've been reminded i come from for all my life (by my parents; by merciless kids at elementary school). only i don't want to come from it.

i'll admit i've never felt like i had the right to the wholesome prize they say lies at the heart of the country where i grew up. just work hard and it's yours; one day you'll be able to call yourself human too.

but at least people don't destroy their own cities back home, right?

except when the power goes out, like it did in New York when i was a kid. there was looting and chaos. people talked about it for years afterwards. i don't remember it except as a blur of fear, the fear of darkness that soaked my early childhood. some of the songs i like mention it.

well, at least the people who rule the country i'm from don't do these kinds of things to people, kill folks cold for being hungry.

Aziz had said he wanted a TV from the hotel, but decided it was too heavy. instead he took a telephone, ripping its cords from the wall. i took a nice white bathrobe with crimson initials on the breast pocket.

and as i'd waited for Aziz to return, i'd stared at this

white wall in a hallway off the hotel's lobby and, struck with the urge to mark it with my name, took a big black marker from behind the front desk—one of the only things of any value behind the desk that someone hadn't already made away with—and written my name (long, curving, sprawling) against the wall, and stood back and admired it. the wall might soon melt to ash, who knew. but in that moment it was mine.

i haven't slept but still feel tireless. 'i have to get to the medina,' i tell Aziz. 'me too,' he says, 'i want to finally go home.' he says that with such a weariness that i wonder if it's been a long, long time since he's been home. though the past day feels like years ago to me, too.

in the cold morning we don't take the quick route, passing the king's palace, but instead pass back through the new town. a gas station is flaming, a whole block consumed by fire, and it looks like a vision of hell. i'm wearing my new gold earrings and the big bathrobe with the hotel's emblem on it, and i have Aziz's telephone underneath it. not very subtle, but it has to do. in front of the gas station—flames filling the sky behind them—are a soldier and a young man. at first we're scared to approach the soldier. we don't look like we are possibly out for any legitimate reason. just looting some exclusive property before the day's work. my heart skips.

it's certainly too late for him not to have seen us, but he seems occupied in taunting the young man. his gun is out. whenever i see one of those, those things i used to dream about— and i've seen so many now, too many—i'm sick to my stomach.

the man, who slightly reminds me of a North African Bob Dylan in that pose, with that smirk, is holding a nice new guitar. probably stolen from a shop nearby. its shiny lacquered wood reflects the glare of the flames. the soldier calls Aziz and me over. *no, just the girl.*

he points the gun at me. frightened out of my mind, i obey. me, the soldier, and Dylan form a wide triangle (fire still raging around us, threatening to swallow us) as Aziz watches from distance.

the soldier speaks to me, loud enough to be heard over the roar of the flames. 'our brother here thought it was a good idea for him to take something that isn't his, to steal it when the seller wasn't even present to defend his property.' i look over to him. he is calm in the face of his fear. the soldier goes on, 'we're going to send him to hell, where thieves go.' he doesn't seem to notice any details about me. i hope he doesn't become interested in sending me to hell, too.

but he does the last thing i'd expect him to do. walks right up to me, and hands me his weapon. it's heavy, and i stumble under the weight of it. says the soldier, 'and we're going to send him to his death in a special way, fit for such a coward: at the hands of a woman.'

the soldier steps back, nods at me, and orders me to shoot the thief. 'what's his name?,' i ask, my voice small, the machine gun heavy.

the thief is unafraid. 'Brahim,' he says with pride, looking back and forth between me and the soldier fiercely. not for one second does this soldier think i'd dare turn this gun on him, so terrified is the whole city of people wearing clothes like him. he's right. i'm trembling terribly, but how can i not obey?

i hoist the gun high. i look Brahim in the eyes. still trembling, trembling, the gun clattering in my hands, the flames leaping higher and closer, i realize this moment as the fulfillment of that fantasy i'd had back home. it's surreal. all i have to do is pull the trigger.

but in my shaking hands the gun drops. it lies on the ground many yards from the soldier. it will take him half a minute to get to the gun, another half a minute to start firing at my back—and i break out into a run, quick, as the flames creep closer to the soldier and Brahim. i trust Aziz to follow me. maybe Brahim will run too.

the telephone falls from underneath my robe and smashes on the ground. i keep running and running. a minute or two away i stop quickly, hands on my knees, to make sure that Aziz is still behind me. he is. i keep running until Beb Boujloud. Aziz stops too.

'let's go to the house of my friend,' i tell him, 'i want to know that she's still alive.'

we spend a mad day twisting through the medina. a distance that on a normal day might take half an hour to walk takes until sundown, past sundown, past horrors, more horrors. on one street i look down and find that my sneakers are mucking through blood that runs on the ground.

i just want to go home. why did my parents send me here? they know their country. don't they love me at all?

we arrive in Your neighborhood, near Beb Fetuah. an area that looks like it's seen the worst of it. i'm glad to be with Aziz, because the dark corners here brood with hints of the kind of raw violence (no metal, just hands, steel-strong with rage) i don't think i'd be able to defend myself from.

we ascend your dark stairs. Aziz seems to know them, in pitch darkness, better than i do. we enter your apartment, whose door is wide open. filled with as many as 30 people inside, moving in trance to the music You make and You stand mouse-eared in your headphones in the midst of it. with a flick of your wrist over the record, the crowd sighs collectively. then You change the beat and they move in frenzy. You're like a puppeteer, controlling the crowd at your whims. orange light from a leather lamp, and madness, and the unlikeliest crowd sweating out their rage.

such power You have. i never would have known, the first day i saw You, so scared, so scarred. i didn't know what You were, but You weren't quite like the rest of us.

You still aren't. but look at You.

3

Look at You. the end of my journey, i'd have thought. only the Sheep that i find is not the Sheep that i lost. not this sorceress in command of a room full of strangers—in command of stranger music.

Aisha (a girl who smashes windows, a girl who points guns) has led me to my own house, to introduce me to You, her friend. where is my sister, whose world i built, and who was my world?

You were the only person i loved since i left the country. before i knew the language here, i could only talk to You. You didn't have words, and we didn't need them. now the voices of these foreign men—voices like beating drums—speak for You. the life i created in this apartment has shifted; where once we revolved around each other, twin planets, You are now at the center of a new dynamic, orbited by many others, the music stringing you all together like gravity.

gone is the girl whose head turned expectantly to hear me coming up the stairs of our apartment, who waited by the door when i entered. gone is the one whose powerlessness gave me courage to seek my own power, and whose loneliness consoled me, my docile Sheep, my lamb.

i approach You. we stand facing each other, looking at one another. i see the joy of recognition in your face. You leave your record table and throw your arms around me. i hug You back, so tight, and everything in the room falls away—all that devilmusic,allthesepeople.thehelli'veseenthesepasttwodays.

the cold agony of that lonely prison.

it all falls away. You're mine again. my sister. my sheep.

You return to your music before the record

plays out. then You play a song for me. i spot Rachid in a corner before i lose myself in the music.

i'm angry at Fes for burning. angry at You for changing. angry at Rachid and Aisha for changing You. i don't care how unjustified. in the morning there's time for me to reclaim everything that's mine. right now i just want to let your unlikely trance wash over me and slip into precious forgetting.

i'm not sure if this new world is still home, but i'll rest in it for now. we all dance, me and Aisha and all these strangers (only Rachid stands apart) until we collapse collectively on the floor after the sun has risen and spread its light like a platter offering the same twin possibility it always will: more of the same struggle, or the relief of hope?

finally, my eyes flutter shut.

For the past two days, as the bread riots raged, You've played your music in vigil, unceasingly, and people have come in and out and danced. the fish seller with his wild beard. the new bride with her henna-stained hands. her new husband, his eyes rimmed with dark kohl.

the old woman from the countryside, bearing between her face's wrinkles the blue-black tattoo lines of her own traditional wedding many years ago. glue-sniffing street boys unaccustomed to being allowed to stay in places where older people gather.

people who need refuge from the danger of the streets but for whom the humiliating defeat of going home (to open and shut the same empty cupboards

to face the same nagging spouse

the same children whose faces crease too young with anger, as they realize there's no escaping the conditions of the world they were unwillingly born to.

the same children asking questions that have no

answers

or just those who want an early start on the task of forgetting that looms on the city's immediate agenda. it's not as laborious as it seems. all you have to do is tell yourself that what your blood had convinced you was true is a lie, that you never saw what you saw, said what you said, heard what you heard. the past isn't fixed—it's a slippery mass that warps to fit your needs for the present, your hopes for the future. people in the city will forget the date, assume it happened a month or so later, next year. what's history anyway, to those excluded from the power to make it? what's time here, anyway, but irrelevant tickmarks on a wall to record the rolling of God's earth, which continues into eternity whether you count it or not?

but though we may get a head start on forgetting, the violence isn't over yet for Fes. this morning royal troops rise up from their occupation of the disputed Sahara especially for the task of stifling our city's anger. a few more weeks of fighting until the passion on all sides is spent and the eagerness to forget overwhelms any legitimate grievances anyone ever had. that's how it always ends when blood fights its own blood. even when they kill each other it's because they've become consumed with love; love too great to be contained by the immutable laws of the world as each assumes them to be, love exploding into death. the king loves his country, a disobedient child that needs chastisement now and then for its own good—lest it take its foolish human dignity into the cruel outside world and be crushed even more finally after learning that, as history's loser, it's not so human as it thought it was. the country loves its king, but cries because out to him because it's yet too young (or too old) to realize that cruelty is not the king's, but the world's, and that this feeling of being crushed is only too tender at the hands of one of its own.

i've kept apart from the crowd the whole time. this music—this foreign beating, pounding, tangled here and there with a rai singer's wail—only makes me feel more apart and makes me hear more piercingly the high pitch of my insurmountable loneliness. i only stay because of You.

i went home to my mother once yesterday, keeping blinders to the sides of my eyes like a workhorse so as not to be permeated by the chaos around me—possible even in war, necessary especially in war. she was frantic in worry for Aisha, who had been missing since the morning it began. she had an urgent message to relay to her, so i came to your place knowing she'd show up here sooner or later.

sure enough Aisha arrived in the early hours of the morning, the time of day when the darkness of the sky begins to lift with light still invisible, the unseen light at a far end of the spectrum that can be felt through the skin as an emotion: hope, just above ultra violet.

she entered wearing the ridiculous white terrycloth bathrobe of the hotel Les Merinides and she entered with, of all people, Aziz. who looked at me less than pleasantly. but the music was loud last night and she was quickly caught up in her dance to your music and i was actually, for a reason i can't explain, nervous to confront Aziz upon his return, and it made me fear to move.

i wait to move, until everyone's asleep but You and me—just heaped on top of one another on the floor—and You're wrapping the cord around your headphones and putting the last records delicately into their sleeves. i watch You. You can't avoid meeting my gaze, and You look up at me. with the makeshift equipment away, You put your arms behind your back and angle yourself against a corner and i become overwhelmed with the kind of love a king has for his nation, like i'm a king and You're my country.

i can help but to move towards You and though You flinch from my breath on your face and my hand on your cheek, i still kiss You. though You struggle beneath my lips i still press them to yours.

and though i feel your heart flutter like a trapped bird i still press my hand to your body, searching for your secret, hoping to find my redemption in You.

i'm sorry. Your eyes close and, your back against the wall, You slip down and away from me, You slink to the ground in sleep with the rest of them, leaving me the last one standing with the salt of remorse on my mouth.

i return to my book, a Palestinian poet. slowly, as morning rises higher into the sky, the people on the floor wake up, gauge the unfamiliarity of their surroundings, shake off sleep, and go home. they each rise in their own peace, noticeably lighter than they had been when they had first wandered into your door a day or two earlier, seeking relief from the heat of the city's anger before it consumed them. after some hours, only You, Aisha, and Aziz are left asleep.

Aisha wakes first, sits up, and blinks her eyes in the new sun. 'Rachid?'

'good morning Aisha.'

she presses her lips together and swallows. 'Rachid, i've seen the most terrible things...'

'i know. i'm sorry,' i say to her, really sincerely, the second apology i've made this morning, 'your parents know what's happening here and they're frantically worried about you. they called my mother and said they want you out of here as soon as possible.'

'...and i think i've done some terrible things.'

'me too,' i tell her, 'but it's the atmosphere. you can't blame yourself.' *i can't blame myself, it's the atmosphere,* 'your parents have bought you a ticket home for tomorrow, so You need to hurry to our house as soon as You can, pack up your things, and get on a train to the airport in Cassablanca.'

'wakha. ok.'

but she's slow to move, still waking.

then Aziz wakes, a few feet from her. he bolts upright and doesn't miss a beat, as though he's dreamed the beginning of the sentence and woke up to finish it, '...and what have you done to my house?,' he asks me. not a hello, but i didn't expect one. the situation these past days cultivates intimacy and makes pleasant introductions irrelevant.

'i've take care of your Sheep.'

'and who is she?,' she asks, pointing to Aisha.

'that's Aisha. you should know, you entered with her last night.'

'i know her name. but how does she know my Sheep? and how does she know my house? and how does she know you?'

'she's my cousin.'

'so you brought her here?'

'yes.'

'to influence my Sheep?'

'to be her friend.'

although the conversation has turned rapid and loud You still lie sleeping the deepest, most dreamless, most bottomless sleep. your chest heaves with breath, but only this distinguishes You from the many lifeless bodies we've all learned to look upon so casually lately.

'so the city's in flames, my life's in ashes, and the closest one to me is no longer herself,' Aziz snarls at my cousin.

'of course she's herself.'

'you don't even know her.'

'i care for her. i was there when you weren't there. i'm sorry.'

'because i asked you to! i trusted you. i didn't ask you to make my house yours.'

'i'm sorry,' says Rachid. someone should tally his

apologies for things he can't help.

'so what do you, do you work?'

'no.'

'because you go to school.'

'no, not anymore.'

'so what, you just sit in another man's house all day, eating his food?'

'with all respect, it's my food now. bought with my money.'

'whose money?'

'my money!'

'*whose* money?'

'my parents' money.'

'exactly. because you're a spoiled rich boy. no wonder you hide indoors. you'd be one of the first ones they look for in this neighborhood, to rip apart limb by limb.'

i know Aziz is penniless. and if this is the one i heard about, the one who asked Rachid to look out for You, i'm sure he's wounded by Rachid's claims. it won't be easy for him to pick up his business after such an absence— people with needs find new ways to fill them quickly. maybe he doesn't know the next time he'll see a dirham.

Sheep, You don't stir. i'm looking at you there, and though the room fills with a cloud of passion, You don't stir from the bliss of your sleep. somehow this is the world You have made, and somehow these are the consequences of borrowing voices from my records to speak for yourself. You have healed weary bodies and lifted some measure of sorrow from some, allowing others to bleed out their anger. but for You, it seems, there is no peace except what is stolen in sleep.

after a stinging silence, i watch something pass over Aziz, a realization that nothing he knew even exists anymore. he speaks in a hushed voice.

The slap of someone's bare feet on the cobblestones below the window beats out a song that calls me down to the street and out into the city again, distracting me from my thoughts. as my mind returns to the room, where You lie sleeping with the deepest peace on the floor, i whisper: 'i'm leaving.'

not forever. but because i cannot decide, i suppose, whether to try to love You or to try to own You—and because this ambivalence sends my head reeling. and because the restlessness that brought me to the city so long ago has gathered in me again, quelled as it was by your strange music for a few hours. i felt this restlessness welling in me in jail. its pace was quickened by the blood on the streets.

i'm as penniless as i was when i arrived in Fes as a country boy. it seems possible that everything i loved in it has disappeared in smoke. i want to try again, to re-enter this apartment and my life with You.

it's not to punish You, that i rise from my seat and turn towards the door. i am angriest, most of all, at time for changing things. maybe when i return—separating myself again from the throng of the hungry, the throng of us who moved to dismantle the city like a swarm of wasps—time will be on my side again.

'Aisha, it was nice to meet you,' i say, shaking her hand as she looks up at me with concern. i go to You and stroke your head. my first and last friend.

the wind whistles hollow up the stairwell, and into the open door. i go, not to beg for my bread, but to take it.

I'm fearful. i hope i mask it well enough. i don't know if i can really take care of You, if You're left to me. Aisha's gone.

i walked her home right after Aziz left. we'd turn to hide behind a corner when a Saharan soldier passes. i still wasn't sure if we were allowed to be outside. i'm still not sure, but it hasn't mattered in a while.

'Aziz didn't touch you, did he? he didn't hurt you?' i wanted to be sure.

'no,' Aisha said, smiling kindly.

'good. he's a dangerous man.'

i told her i had decided to go back to the university this upcoming term. 'i'm useless without it,' i'd said.

'that's really great,' she told me, 'Khalti will be so proud of you.'

i left Aisha framed by my parents' doorway. i knew she wastryingtosparemehersentimentalitybykeepinghergoodbye brief: 'we'll see each other,' was all she said. she smiled at me. i'll miss her courage. was all the courage i thought i had hers?

that morning Aziz left and i left Aisha, You slept for two days straight. and i stayed with You, lifting You to a banquette and covering You with a wool blanket.

when You woke, your eyes, finally open, were empty. something in them had gone. now it's been a few more days. Aziz must have known, when he conceded the victory to me, that to do so was to utterly defeat me.

still i'm faithful to you, even when you are no longer faithful to yourself.

everyone's gone, even the light in your eyes in gone, and i'm faithful to You.

yesterday You shat in a corner of the room. You

actually defecated on the floor, twice now, and i found it, and i cleaned it, my head reeling with the foul smell and the absolute and total horror of it.

now You refuse to walk upright. i pull you to your feet, holding my mouth tight to keep from wailing—my cheek to your cheek, i'm pouring hot tears into your ears, my mouth dark and slick, my nose dripping. i want to scream at You. i scream at You! *be yourself, why can't you be yourself?*

You're just a body. You've left me. are you punishing me?

but i loved You.

i pull you to your feet, but You slip down, You slide to the floor. i collapse onto the banquette. i sleep, forgetting that i fell asleep until i realize that I'm waking up—and You're crawling across the floor on your hands and knees, looking for food. what about your music, then? but i don't have a clue about how to work the turntables to bring the sounds You loved to You. and i can't see that there is anything to salvage within you. in my arms i carry You a long distance, just to the outskirts of the city. i want to reach into my past and start again. You were never what i thought You were. You were sick. rejected by the world. if i ever identified with that i was mistaken. if i ever thought that You—this thing limp and half-human in my arms —were some kind of ideal i should reach for, then i was sick too. i can only pray that i'm better. i'll press forward and make something of myself.

i'll leave You here, away from the city. not far from here, the city burns its trash. here's a patch of grass. i can't do anything for You. You'll be better on your own than You ever could have been with me.

i turn away from You, to face the city, to go back into it and on with my life, forgetting—as we must—what needs to be forgotten.

i look back at You there in the grass. You look at

me, a sheep's brown eyes. i can't leave You there. i shuffle towards You. i try to touch You but You shrink from me. don't You know what's good for You? i try to lift You but You resist me with such strength as i've never seen from You— and the shock of feeling this sudden strength from your body causes me to let You go, to lift my hands in surrender.

then, You run. all four limbs tearing at the ground, widening the distance between us until You recede into it, never looking back. i watch You as You pause at the top of a hill. and i turn around to walk across the field and over scraps of metal and plastic peeking from the earth. i find the gravel road, drag my feet across it, climb into a taxi, and go home. and i go back to my classes. i imagine they'll clear the streets of debris and wash the blood from them. they'll fill the hollow windows with glass. the mud will be mixed for new plaster, to re-form any building that crumbled, any wall partitioned. the city never dies. the city will live again.

we can't imagine how many times the same scene has been repeated in time. a few years ago when the price of bread went up the city had cried out. i remember; and just like this time the city had been silenced. Fes is as old as Earth, and like Earth prone to periodic tremors, occasional eruptions of fire from its belly. if the riots seem singular, it's only because we don't have Fes' scope. we think time is a line, start to finish. you live for a time and then you're erased. but for Fes time is a curve, a circle. we're small in it. what happened before will happen again. the streets will erupt again, the streets will be quieted. the bodies covered in dirt, buried in the old garden of kings, rare flowers to be pruned around the bones. the bodies covered in dirt, buried quietly. the bodies buried without names. the bodies dumped in heaps.

the bodies buried secretly, in the sand of the desert, in fields by the sea. the mothers whose sons disappear, as though they never were. white bones peeking from the soil like tender shoots. white bones bleached in the cruel sun of the Sahara.

some of my classmates: never were.

some of my neighbors: never were.

even now i know it—already. only after years will the disappearance turn into assumed death. in our ways, we all die; but the city lives again.

Sheep, You never were. You never were. i erase You—like the mighty hand of the state i erase You.

As the city cools, so do i. i'd flung myself to the city's rage. i lost myself in the city, destroying it—moving as though in a dream across days now locked away for me, conveniently, by that quiet, tidy steward of the mind who keeps us from ourselves so that we can continue.

even though You are not here when i return, i do choose to continue. do You think i would have survived all that flame, all that blood, and my own anger besides, if i hadn't been sustained by You? not only by your memory but by the hope that i would return to You, still. for so long, this memory and this hope have been realer to me than the world i wake to. they will be enough to ease me back home.

covered in ash, i returned to the apartment. i twisted the door open. it was mid-afternoon, the pale winter sky bright through the window's iron bars. where i had hoped to find You waiting, the ghost of You in my memory's eye shimmered, then faded.

one of my former clients, who raised chickens, had given me five eggs and a sound pat on the back when he saw that i'd returned. so i went to the tank of butane, lit it, and boiled an egg. i peeled it and, salting it as i ate, took small bites of it until the sun, like the round egg, also began to wane.

i waited. as You must have waited for me, those months. i had come to a resolution, winding again down the route to our house, or maybe climbing the stairs, or maybe the dream of rage i'd lived for the past few days had reconciled me to it, like when you go to sleep with a difficult problem and wake with the answer. i was prepared to accept a Sheep who had changed with time, as i myself had probably changed. so i had come up the steep stairs with nervous anticipation. we would begin our life again. we would come to re-learn each other.

biting for the egg, my teeth now scraped my fingers. the house was still empty. the sun went down, and still i was alone. where were You? as night came, i flicked on the single light bulb hanging from its wire and the cracked white plaster walls were illuminated. the house was clean, the few things in it tidy: a record player with records stacked neatly next to it, benches for sitting, a floor mat of woven plastic. half an hour after dark a woman knocked on the door. she seemed surprised to find me behind it. 'i saw the light was on,' she apologized. her shyness made me smile. 'who were you expecting to find?,' i asked her, my voice inflecting that it was absurd of her to be surprised when the owner of a home answered its door.

the woman, whose mournful eyebrows gave her face its only weight, looked to her feet. 'i thought it would have been nice to hear some music tonight.' it strikes me that she has come looking for You.

'sister,' i tell her, 'i'm afraid we're both missing the same person.'

'forgive me,' she says. i offer her a glass of tea, sure that she will decline, that sitting alone with a strange man is a dangerous idea for her. but from the doorway she spots Aisha's record player. 'does it still play?,' she asks me, and i turn my head to follow her pointed finger.

'i don't know. i've never really touched one of those things.'

boldening, the woman—my downstairs neighbor, whose

name i tried to place—stepped over the threshold. 'do you think we could try?,' she asked.

so, after she had fumbled with taking a record from its sleeve and putting it on to play, we listened. and as these sounds from another city expanded against the familiar walls of the house, i realized that i had inherited a world from You. i had also, perhaps, inherited a community. my neighbor and i sipped tea without a word, the smell of mint rising in steam around our cupped hands.

sitting there in my house again my mind couldn't help but to turn to practical concerns. i had no idea what to expect, with the morning that would come. i'm on the edge of something new again, something wide open. will i become what i was, or something else? if i don't rebuild my business—reconnecting with the desires of my clients, and riding into the mountains once a week to bring back salve to satisfy them—then will i re-make myself as something new? 'perhaps she was a ghost,' the neighbor offers out of her silence, 'and not of this world? i know people who say she wasn't real, sure as she was before her eyes.' 'of course she's real,' i tell her.

if tomorrow comes and i am without You, if tomorrow passes into days and weeks, if guilt for having left You begins to creep into me, if fear for your safety enters me, if anger at having been abandoned by You does—i will remember that we create ourselves from nothing, You and i, we magicians. i will remind myself of your self-sufficiency, and my own, something we share even across distance. in these ways i will begin: defending your rumor and tending your community like a good shepherd, and making my own new paths across this city. as the city builds itself from its cinders, so will i. we come from nothing, and we return to nothing. this is what i know. it is the one thing i have to tell You, because i know You already understand it. it's the truth we share. and it's why, still without

You, i don't worry. we lay ourselves out upon a blank world.

And that city behind me? the place that remembered me
to myself? i have no words for it. i'm as silent as You are.
at the kitchen table in Brooklyn, where my father had once
slunk in his seat, defeated by his daughter's failure, i will
reach to hold his hand. i'll tell him i know who he is. a month
from now, on the tiny TV in the kitchen, he and i will watch
the missiles of our country (our country? which one?) fly
into Baghdad and i'll feel the one last sliver of innocence
rise out me, and i'll nod in homage to it as it goes out an
ear and escapes into the atmosphere. what i'll be left with
is a sober residue: knowing that half the world has been
burning while i was distracted by the life in front of me.
what does that make us, then, my father and me? veterans,
lucky survivors with our humanity—and our guilt—intact.
i forgot my records at Your apartment. at home again in
my room, i slowly begin to replace them with cassette tapes
recorded from the radio, vigilant for my favorite songs, songs
that remind me of You, with my ear against the speaker.

i might just show up to school every day this semester,
and maybe when i see Rachid again we'll both have new
diplomas—on that faraway day, God knows how far away.
somehow i know that You won't be there. i was afraid for You
when i left, didn't want to leave You there curled sleeping. but
i gather some courage and hope for You, and will You to be ok.

i see You, curiously, on all fours. in a pasture. eating
weeds. strange image, but i know You're free there. when
the rain comes, You huddle under a tree. when the wind
comes, You withstand it. You live to survive impossible
things, like You always have (abandonment, friendlessness,
motherlessness, inhumanity: these impossible things).
You give yourself a name, a name with no syllables. You
sing to yourself, songs with no sounds, and we hear You.

Acknowledgements

Sincerest thanks to Karima and Omar of Fes, Morocco for the gift of their friendship; may our knowing one another always bear good fruit. Thanks also to Mohammed Alami Chentoufi for sitting down and sharing with me, and likewise to Si Abdelnabi of the American Language Center in Fes. Thank you to MACECE of Rabat and to the Fulbright Commission for funding the research and language study that made this work possible. Thank you to the late bell hooks and to E. Ethelbert Miller for encouraging early readers. Opal Moore, thanks for mentorship, examining this work's ethical lens and for your continuing example. Thanks to Currun Singh and Laura Jo Hess and the others of the book's first readers. Parts of this novella appeared in *Transitions* in 2012 as "Always a Watcher" and in *Aunt Chloe: A Journal of Artful Candor* as "The Body's Betrayal" and I thank these publications. I am grateful to everyone in *Fes* who welcomed me into their homes and city and gave me their trust and care. So many friends and family members supported me through their faith in this work over the years and all are in my heart for holding and keeping me, and for believing with me in this work so that I could continue until it saw light.

About the Author

Chantal James received a Fulbright fellowship in creative writing that allowed her to live in Morocco researching and writing *Fes is a Mirror*. James learned the local Arabic dialect to conduct interviews from eyewitnesses to its political events for the book. Her novel excerpt, *Upon Alleyways*, was featured in *Black Fire This Time, Vol 2*. Her debut novel *NONE BUT THE RIGHTEOUS* was chosen as one of Kirkus' 10 most anticipated fiction books of the year and was one of *Library Journal*'s top winter debuts. James has been published across genres—as a poet, fiction writer, essayist, and book reviewer—in such venues as *The New Republic, Catapult, Paste Magazine*, Harvard's *Transition Magazine* (where an excerpt of *Fes is a Mirror* appeared), *The Bitter Southerner* and more.

James' honors include a Fulbright, a finalist position for the Alex Albright Creative Nonfiction prize from the North Carolina Literary Review for 2019, and a fellowship to the Vermont Studio Center.

* 9 7 9 8 2 1 8 8 4 3 7 2 4 *